THE LOST COAST

The Revenge of Mad River Billy

By

DANIEL ROBINSON

The Lost Coast

Daniel Robinson

Disclaimer

This is a work of fiction. Names, characters, places, and events are either products of the author's imagination or used fictitiously. Any resemblance to actual persons, living or dead, events, or locales is purely coincidental.

While some elements may be inspired by real-life locations or historical events, they have been altered, exaggerated, or entirely reimagined for the sake of storytelling and artistic expression.

The opinions and viewpoints expressed by the characters do not reflect those of the author, publisher, or any affiliated entities. The author and publisher make no claims regarding the accuracy or factuality of the content in this novel. This book is intended for entertainment purposes only, and any actions taken based on its content are at the reader's discretion and risk.

Dedication

This book is dedicated to my family and friends who have encouraged me to be creative through story telling. I especially want to give a shout out to my grandchildren whose overwhelming love and affection keeps me smiling:

Sean, Rylan, Jackson, Juliana, Scarlett, Noah, Nova, and baby Lucas – and to those yet to come! I love you all.

Poppy

Table of Contents

Daniel Robinson

CHAPTER 1

The Massacre

February 26ᵗʰ, 1860
Annual Wiyot Renewal Ceremonies
Indian Island,
Humboldt County, California

Jacob Hurley's hand trembled as he gripped the hatchet. The morning was cool, yet sweat trickled down his spine, soaking the fabric of his cotton shirt. Smoke and fear hung in the air, their oppressive weight pressing down on him as he crouched in the underbrush. Dim light from dying fires barely illuminated the outlines of his companions, blending them into the shadows like ghosts.

Thirty men, handpicked for their supposed loyalty and strength, formed a loose circle around him. His father, Timothy Hurley, would lead the attack. And though only a few feet away, Jacob could barely see him, the emotional distance between them far greater than the physical.

Knives, hatchets, and axes gleamed faintly in the moonlight, ready for slaughter. The group left their firearms behind—a calculated choice to prevent gunshots from alerting the Wiyot tribe. Razor-sharp steel being their weapon of choice. A few men grumbled, but Timothy's unyielding authority silenced any objections. No one dared question his decisions.

At just shy of twenty, Jacob never killed another human being, nor did he want to. The thought of what lay ahead filled him with dread. He begged to stay home, but his father insisted he "be a man" and do the right thing. Unfortunately, doing the right thing apparently meant slaughtering every native on Indian Island.

The cold steel of the knife and hatchet in Jacob's hands leeched the warmth from his body, leaving him shivering with trepidation. He struggled with the imminent act, haunted by the thought of the Wiyot tribe's innocence, particularly the women and children. How could his father expect him to deliver death to these people? What had they done to him?

The seeds of this night were sown weeks earlier in secret meetings held in the dim back room of the general store. Timothy Hurley had rallied the settlers, fanning the flames of anger and resentment that simmered beneath the surface of their community. Beside him stood Dylan Frazier, Ezra Taylor, Arnold "Arnie" Johnson, Frank Tyson, the Blanton brothers— Don and Fred—Deacon Howard, and David Tucker. Together, they crafted the plan, each man adding his voice to the rhetoric until the idea of massacre seemed not only acceptable but inevitable.

Stovepipe Peterson, an aging trapper with a penchant for storytelling, reminded the group about the Wiyots' annual World Renewal Ceremony. "They gather on Indian Island every year, the whole damn tribe," he had said, his voice gravelly with years of tobacco use. "They sing, they chant. They eat and they drink—and they drink a lot. It's the perfect time to strike."

The others nodded, their expressions grim. To them, the ceremony was an affront, a reminder of a way of life they sought to erase. Timothy had seized on the idea, declaring it their duty to act. "We'll hit them when they're all together, unarmed and unsuspecting. It'll be quick and clean."

Jacob attended those meetings, though he said little. Any protests offered had fallen on deaf ears, drowned out by the collective fervor of men convinced they were doing God's work.

A whistle, low and sharp, sliced through the stillness. The signal to move out given. The men around Jacob began advancing, silent as predators stalking their prey. His boyhood friend, Henry Thomas, advanced on his left, a grin of anticipation plastered on his face. "Bet I get more of those heathens than you do, farm boy," he whispered, elbowing Jacob.

Jacob swallowed hard; his throat dry. "Bet you do, too," he murmured, though his voice barely carried above a whisper. His hands trembled, the hatchet in his grip feeling heavier with each step.

As they neared the edge of the encampment, the first teepees came into view. Shapes moved within, silhouetted by the faint glow of dying fires. The Wiyot tribe was unaware, their trust in the sanctity of the ceremony leaving them defenseless.

Jacob's mind raced. He needed a way out. If he fell behind, his father would notice and push him forward. But what if he slipped away unnoticed? He could hide until the attack ended. Risky, he knew, but better to hide than participating in the massacre.

As the others advanced, Jacob slowed his pace until the darkness swallowed him. He slipped into a recess behind a hut, his heart pounding so hard he thought he might faint. The rest of the men were out of sight now, but the sounds of killing would reach him soon.

It began quietly. Dylan Frazier and Ezra Taylor entered a teepee, the inhabitants still asleep. Taylor tripped over a cooking pot, startling one of the women. "What are you doing here?" she cried in the Wiyot tongue.

Ezra sneered. "You even talk like a heathen," he spat before bringing a mallet down on her skull, silencing her instantly. Frazier followed, hacking at two children with his axe, their small bodies offering no resistance.

The two men exited the tepee, their lust for blood only beginning. They saw two women holding babies trying to flee. Without a word between them, Frazier went left while Taylor went right. They did a classic pincher move and caught the two escaping women mid stride. Both went down with death blows. The babies received no reprieve.

Similar scenes played out across the village. Men burst into teepees and huts, their blades flashing as they cut down the unarmed and unaware. Screams filled the air, rising in a crescendo of terror and pain. The settlers' initial attempts at stealth gave way to chaos as they reveled in the slaughter, howling like beasts.

Though anarchy reined all around him, the young Hurley cowered in the shadows of a tribal hut. He gaped in revulsion as the settlers struck with a ferocity that defied their human form, attacking anything that moved.

Among them was his father—the gentle parent who raised him with kindness, now a symbol of that rage. Witnessing what felt like a betrayal of everything he believed, Jacob experienced a despair so profound he knew he would never be the same.

"God forgive us," Jacob whispered, his voice trembling. He wanted nothing more than to be anywhere but there. Like a frightened turtle retreating into its shell, he slid deeper into the hut's dark crevice, yearning for invisibility. But his fragile sense of safety was shattered by a scream—primal and full of pain. Blinking in confusion, Jacob turned just in time to see a bloodied Wiyot boy, no older than thirteen, charging toward him with a knife. The boy's face revealed a mask of fury, his eyes blazing with defiance.

The sight jolted Jacob from his despair, survival overtaking paralysis. As the Indian boy neared, Jacob's weapon—a hatchet not meant for this grim purpose—flew from his hands in a reflex of pure instinct, its deadly arc ending with a sickening thud. The sharpened blade of the steel head cleaved the attacker's skull, dropping him dead in his tracks, his body slamming to the ground in a cloud of dust. Jacob's eyes bulged in horror.

"God almighty, what have I done?" the boy sobbed. Collapsing to his knees, he covered his face with his hands, his sobs coming in gasping, uncontrolled heaves. Despite the death and destruction around him, he was oblivious. The invisibility he desired now complete, though not in the way he hoped.

After what felt like an eternity, Jacob removed his hands and ventured a tentative look. The Indian boy lay unmoving, his lifeless eyes staring blankly. The top of his head was a gory mess, with flesh and brain matter exposed. Jacob screamed, retched, and vomited. He would have stayed there until the killing ended, or until someone killed him—it didn't matter any longer.

"Get up boy. What the hell are you doing down there, you want to get yourself killed," Deacon Howard yelled at the slumping Hurley. "Now get up, pull that axe out of that heathen's head, and follow me."

The mournful boy not only got up and followed Howard, but he also followed him in carrying out the destruction he so desperately wanted to avoid. He was now a killer like all the rest. This was something he would never be able to come to terms with for the rest of his life. And in time, another would make sure he would remember too.

CHAPTER 2

The Curse of Mad River Billy

Before the sun crested the eastern horizon, the massacre was over. More than two hundred Wiyot lay dead or dying, their peaceful village reduced to smoldering ruin. The settlers, their bloodlust momentarily sated, surveyed the carnage. The ground was littered with broken bodies, crimson pools soaking into the soil where children had played hours earlier. Smoke curled lazily from the remnants of teepees; their skeletal frames silhouetted against the pale morning sky.

Among the attackers, there were only a handful of minor injuries. For these men, it was a triumphant victory. Yet, beneath the bravado, unease stirred. The sight of so much death, even to men who had wielded the blades, clung to them like an unwelcome shadow.

Near the center of the village, two survivors were dragged from a makeshift hiding place: a woman clutching a terrified young girl. The settlers encircled them like vultures around carrion, jeering and shoving. The captives were brought before Timothy Hurley, the orchestrator of the attack.

"It's your call, Hurley," Dylan Frazier said, nudging the trembling woman with the butt of his axe. "You planned this. You get the honors."

Timothy gripped his hunting knife, his chest rising and falling as he stared at the captives. His breath came in ragged gasps, his face slick with sweat and blood. Without hesitation, he seized the child by her hair. The girl whimpered, her small body trembling, but she made no attempt to pull away. With one swift motion, Hurley drew the blade across her throat.

Her dying body crumpled to the ground.

Just as Hurley slid his knife across the women's throat, a sharp cry echoed from the edge of the clearing. The settlers froze, their heads snapping toward the sound. From the trees emerged a lone figure, his silhouette tall and commanding.

It was Kinetitah, known to the settlers as Mad River Billy, the Wiyot shaman. His eyes widened in horror as he took in the scene—the blood, the bodies, the lifeless child at Hurley's feet. Then his gaze landed on the woman, blood pouring from the gaping wound at her neck.

"Áa hágilh!" Billy's voice broke like thunder. His language was incomprehensible to most of the settlers, but his grief was unmistakable.

Hurley's head snapped up, his bloodied hands tightening on the knife. For a moment, their eyes met across the field of devastation. Billy's burned with rage and sorrow. Hurley's were alight with cold, grim satisfaction. He released the woman's head letting her fall to the ground.

"You will pay for what you have done," the shaman screamed, his voice carrying across the blood-soaked ground. "You and yours will forever feel my wrath. Watch now as I call upon the bringer of death and know this, you can never hide or escape, nor will you ever be able to stop his revenge."

The settlers, now gathered around Hurley, exchanged uneasy glances. Dylan Frazier's smirk faltered. Ezra Taylor shifted his weight, gripping his mallet tighter. Even Frank Tyson, known for his ruthless efficiency, took a step back as Billy raised his hands to the sky and began to wildly chant.

"What's he doing?" Fred Blanton whispered.

"Shut up," Hurley hissed, his knuckles white on his knife.

Billy's words were rhythmic and fierce, spoken in the Wiyot tongue. His arms moved in intricate patterns, drawing invisible lines in the air. The settlers watched Billy's tirade with a mixture of humor, awe, and unease until Hurley decided to end it.

With murderous intent, the group's leader stepped toward the shaman. After all, there could be no witnesses. But the blood-splattered killer stopped short when the shaman let out a ferocious shriek. With eyes ablaze in hatred, Billy crashed his hands together over his head. A blinding flash of light erupted from his palms, forcing Hurley to stumble back.

When the light faded, Billy stood tall, his eyes glowing with an otherworldly intensity. "You have been cursed!" the shaman proclaimed, his voice heavy with the weight of his people's suffering. "The shadows of our fallen will haunt your dreams. Terror will fester in your souls for decades. And know this: the heritage you have tried to erase tonight will outlast your own.

"As you have killed our children yours will die, never to see children of their own! And just as you have destroyed our family's legacies, yours will end when the last of your kin is devoured."

Hurley recovered his footing, his jaw tightening. "Enough of this nonsense." He reached for his axe, but Billy was already moving. With one last glare, the shaman turned and sprinted toward the bay. The settlers gave chase, but the Indian dove into the water, disappearing beneath the surface.

For a long moment, the men stood in stunned silence, the weight of his curse pressing on them like an invisible hand. Then Hurley shook his head, his expression hardening.

"Burn it all," he barked. "Leave nothing."

The settlers set to work, torching the remnants of the village and piling bodies into the flames. The air grew thick with the stench of burning flesh, a smell that would linger in their minds long after the smoke had cleared.

CHAPTER 3

No Justice for the Fallen

Billy emerged sometime later upon the shores of Eureka. Exhausted and drenched, he stumbled into the town square, drawing curious stares. By the time he reached the sheriff's office, a small crowd had followed.

Once facing the lawman, he began relating tales of the massacre. His voice, though careful in its delivery, carried the weight of accusation, naming those who had stained their hands with Wiyot blood.

"Sheriff, I've given you the names of the leaders. I recognized all of them, but there are many more. You must do something. They are murderers," Billy exclaimed as he faced the sheriff of Eureka.

"Now hold on there, Billy, you're making some very dangerous accusations. What proof do you have?" Sheriff Freeman warned.

"What proof? My people are all dead. Killed by the men who live here. Their leader is Timothy Hurley, and I watched him kill my sister and niece."

"Well, that's what you say. But no one else has come forth to corroborate your story. Bring me one other person who saw what happened, and I'll bring the lot in," the sheriff declared, a patronizing grin on his face.

Billy's jaw tightened. "There are none. Haven't you been listening? They killed everyone. I'm all that's left."

Freeman sighed, leaning back again. "That's too bad. Without other witnesses, I'm afraid there's nothing I can do."

Billy's hands clenched into fists. "You're letting murderers go free. Have you no morals?"

"Boy, I'm not sure who you think you're talking to right now, but I suggest you get out before I lock you up."

Billy stormed out, his heart heavy with rage and despair. The crowd with him had swelled. Now, a hundred or more had gathered as he reached the town square. It was his chance to persuade the people of Eureka. Standing on a platform, he raised his voice one last time.

"They think they've silenced me," he began, his voice steady but filled with a quiet fury. "They think the blood they've spilled will wash away the Wiyot people. But they are wrong."

Grumblings broke out by several bystanders, but Billy pressed on, his voice rising. "The earth remembers. The spirits remember. The blood of my sister, my niece, and my people cry out for justice."

Someone from the crowd scoffed. "Justice? There's nothing left of your tribe to seek justice! Let it go, or you will be next."

Billy's eyes burned as he turned to the speaker. "Let it go? You dare to speak of forgetting? I do not forget. The spirits do not forget. And I will not let those who did this terrible thing forget, nor will their descendants be free of my retribution.

"I will call upon the ancient powers of the Wiyot. Soon, a beast, born of vengeance and sorrow, a creature with no mercy in its heart will appear. It will rise, hunting those tied to the blood spilled on Tuluwat Island. And on the hundredth anniversary…" His voice dropped, and the crowd leaned in to hear. "The last surviving descendants of the murderers will perish. Every. Last. One."

A ripple of unease passed through the settlers. Some laughed nervously, dismissing his words as the ravings of a deranged lunatic. But others exchanged uneasy glances, the weight of his curse settling into their bones.

Billy raised his arms, his voice now thunderous. "You may not believe today, but soon the killers will, as will their children and grandchildren. The beast will remind them. It will not stop until justice is done."

With that, Mad River Billy turned and walked away, leaving the townspeople to grapple with the chilling proclamation.

Kinetitah returned to Tuluwat Island, determined to fulfill his vow. There were things he needed, ancient spiritual relics—and he knew where to find them. At the ancestral burial grounds, he unearthed the bones of the tribe's previous shaman. With care, he removed the skeletal hands, now long stripped of flesh, and collected remnants of the deceased: hair, fingernails, toenails, and four teeth—two from the upper jaw and two from the lower. Within the grave, he uncovered ritual artifacts, including rare herbs, spices, and vials of animal blood, all of which he stored in a satchel tied at his waist.

From the remains, Billy also retrieved an amulet crafted from an owl's skull and a small pouch containing four stones: onyx, moonstone, moss agate, and jasper, polished smooth by years of use by past shamans. Finally, resting on the shaman's chest, he found a sacrificial knife, which he reverently added to his collection.

With the items secured, he traveled south to a secluded coastal area he had visited with his father as a child. While the Wiyot people primarily worshipped on mountaintops, they also revered a network of caves believed to hold extraordinary powers. In these sacred spaces, Billy planned to summon the enigmatic forces he had encountered in his youth, channeling their energy to carry out his dark vow of vengeance.

The settlers called him Mad River Billy, a name born of mockery and misunderstanding, but to the Wiyot people, he was Kinetitah. From the moment he could speak, his family knew there was something extraordinary about him. Kinetitah had a gift—or perhaps a curse. He could see things others could not, sense events before they unfolded. His insight was uncanny, leaving even the elders uneasy at times.

The tribe's shamanka recognized his gifts and convinced his parents to let her train him, hoping to guide and develop his abilities. Though hesitant, they agreed.

Kinetitah learned quickly, mastering the use of herbs and rituals to heal wounds and soothe pain. These practical skills were impressive, but what awed the shamanka most were his visions. He described events with startling clarity—scenes of past transgressions, whispers of future tragedies. These weren't dreams; they were vivid experiences, delivered with such conviction that even the skeptics among the tribe were forced to take notice.

One day, after visiting two pregnant women in her care, the shamanka returned to her tent, where Kinetitah awaited her. Without prompting, the boy spoke: "They will both have daughters. One will have eyes like the sky and the earth—one blue, one brown." He was nine. The prediction, like so many of his, came true.

At eleven, he warned a hunter: "When face the beast, swim. Don't fight." The man was puzzled by the cryptic advice until weeks later when he surprised a mountain lion and her grown cub. Cornered by the animals on the banks of a river, the hunter remembered Kinetitah's words. He leaped into the water, narrowly escaping death.

By thirteen, Kinetitah's abilities had begun to frighten even himself. One day, he vanished without warning, taking no food, water, or tools. When he failed to return, the tribe sent searchers into the woods. They found him over a mile from the village, sitting cross-legged in the dirt, rocking back and forth. His hands were bloodied, his face pale, his eyes unfocused.

The braves cautiously approached. Kinetitah's eyes were rolled back, his hair tangled, his face pale, and his hands bloody. Leaves and dirt clung to his clothes, and he looked utterly drained. When they spoke to him, it was as if he couldn't hear them.

Then, without warning, he began speaking—to someone or something invisible. His voice rose and fell, shifting between speech, grunts, and animalistic sounds. At times, he laughed loudly and with unsettling joy, and then his speech would alter to sorrow and pain. Just as suddenly as it started, it stopped, and Kinetitah emerged from the trance, bewildered but aware.

One of the braves asked him who he had been speaking to. Kinetitah calmly gave a name and described the man in vivid detail. But no one in the group recognized the person he described. When they returned to the village, the braves recounted the incident, including the boy's claim of speaking to someone who wasn't there.

During a gathering of the elders, Kinetitah admitted he had never heard of the man before. Yet, he described him in remarkable detail, down to the bright beads and shells on his clothing. According to Kinetitah, the man explained that he had been hunting along the coast when a pack of coyotes attacked and killed him. The boy described the exact location where the remains could be found.

Two elders recalled a tribesman who had disappeared many years before Kinetitah's birth. He had gone hunting and never returned. Acting on the boy's account, three braves traveled to the site he described. There, they found human bones, confirming Kinetitah's story.

Years passed, and Kinetitah's reputation grew. When he was seventeen, the village chief approached him, desperate for answers. His prized stallion had vanished. Kinetitah performed the expected rituals but already knew the truth. He had seen the horse in a vision on the day it disappeared. In the dream, a tribal teen took the horse, hoping to absorb the chief's wisdom by riding it. However, the steed stumbled and broke its leg. The boy, fearing punishment, left it to die and never spoke of what he did.

Kinetitah provided the exact location of the horse's body and described how it died. The chief sent searchers to look, and when they returned, every detail was as the boy foretold. Though the chief was grateful, the incident left the tribe wary. They began to wonder if Kinetitah's visions were a blessing—or something far darker.

The question of his power would come to a head on his twenty-fifth birthday, a day that coincided with the tribe's annual World Renewal Ceremony. Held on sacred Tuluwat Island, the ceremony was a time of joy and spiritual reflection, meant to cleanse the earth and ensure harmony among all living things. The tribe believed that during certain rituals and ceremonies, the life forces of those interred would inhabit the current shaman's body.

During that year's celebration, Kinetitah reveled in the festivities and the tribe's acknowledgment of his birthday. However, by late afternoon, he began to feel peculiar. His head ached, his vision blurred, and his hearing dulled until he could no longer hear his people singing or talking. Unsure of what was happening, he quietly slipped away to the same secluded area in the woods where he had gone as a thirteen-year-old. He hoped to rest and recover, but his condition worsened.

Sitting cross-legged on the ground, Kinetitah closed his eyes and concentrated on clearing his mind. After a moment, he started an incoherent chant while rocking back and forth. Abruptly, his head snapped back, his eyes rolled in their sockets, and his body began to tremble violently. He fell onto his back and went into a deep, sleeplike trance.

As he lay on the damp earth, Kinetitah experienced several intense dreams. In one vision, the ocean churned with restless power. Orca whales surfaced and dove in unison, their movements deliberate, almost ritualistic. They lifted their bodies from the water, seemingly ensuring he was watching, then dove back down before breaching again, leaping majestically into the air and crashing down with explosive splashes.

Seals and walruses flanked Kinetitah, barking and growling in approval of the showing. Behind him, a dozen black bears and a pack of wild coyotes bobbed their heads up and down while howling in appreciation. The scene was a mesmerizing symphony of sights and sounds.

At that moment, the scene shifted as a naked white man emerged from the woods. The man carried a large knife and hatchet in his hands. He stared at Kinetitah but didn't acknowledge his presence. The man turned back toward the trees and put his finger to his lips.

He motioned to his left and then his right. Like phantoms, dozens of armed men appeared. They walked up to the unmoving animals and began hacking away. As they struck, the animals transformed into humans—but not just humans—his own Wiyot villagers.

The scene was a bloodbath. Kinetitah stood frozen, unable to move as he watched the slaughter unfold. His anger raged beyond control, and suddenly, his body changed. His arms and legs morphed, bulging and expanding while growing massive claw-like appendages. Kinetitah screamed in agony, though the sound was more of a monstrous roar.

His skin bubbled and crystallized into scale-like formations. He grew in height and width, towering nearly fifteen feet tall. His eyes became glowing red orbs, and his mouth was filled with rows of jagged, razor-sharp teeth. He was terrifying in every way. The attackers watched in horror, and before they could flee, the creature struck. The slaughter of the Wiyots evolved into the slaughter of the white intruders.

When Kinetitah awoke from the stupor, he was exhausted and covered in blood, though he bore no wounds. Returning to the festival, he recounted the vision to the shamanka and several elders. After hearing his tale, the oldest elder gasped and whispered, "Puchúri-ghúrru—the Destroyer."

Little did Kinetitah know, but this dream would be more than a dream…

CHAPTER 4

The Birth of the Beast

Under a moonless sky, Mad River Billy crouched near the edge of an ancient, weather-beaten cave deep within the coastal wilderness. The flickering light of a small fire danced on the damp walls, casting eerie shadows that moved like ghosts of a forgotten past.

This cave, hidden beneath towering cliffs and known only to a few, was where he would invoke the dark ritual that would forever alter his fate.

Once the shaman of the Wiyot tribe, Kinetitah was now an exile. Driven by vengeance and the unquenchable need to avenge his slaughtered family, he had returned to this hallowed place to do what no shaman dared—transform himself into a creature of unrelenting wrath.

Before him lay a circle of artifacts—each retrieved from the graves of his ancestors. Two skeletal hands from a longdead shaman, a ceremonial knife with a blade chipped from obsidian, a pouch of sacred stones polished smooth from centuries of handling, and an amulet fashioned from the skull of an owl—the symbol of wisdom and death. Around the circle, herbs and potions simmered in clay bowls, releasing the acrid stench of burnt sage, wolfsbane, and nightshade.

The fumes hung thick in the cave, filling it with a darkness that was more than the absence of light.

Kinetitah's hands trembled as he dipped his fingers into a bowl filled with animal blood—wolf, bear, and eagle—the most powerful predators of the land, chosen to imbue him with their strength, ferocity, and vision. He painted his face in streaks of red, black, and white, each line a symbol of death, war, and transformation.

He took a deep breath and recited ancient incantations, his voice low and guttural. Every word was a summoning of spirits long forgotten. The fire flared, growing brighter as if the spirits of the cave were awakening.

He picked up the owl skull amulet, pressing it to his forehead, feeling the cold, smooth surface against his skin. It was said the owl could see into the darkness of men's hearts, and Kinetitah needed that vision now. As he closed his eyes, he saw them—the settlers who had stormed his village with knives and hatchets, their faces twisted in hatred as they butchered his people, his family. He saw his sister's lifeless body and his young niece's blood staining the earth. He witnessed the fire, the smoke, the screams.

Rage surged within him, hot and fierce.

Kinetitah reached for the shaman's bones, the skeletal hands that had once wielded great power. He positioned them in the circle and poured a vial of animal blood over the bony fingers, watching as the crimson liquid seeped into the crevices. The bones absorbed the blood and began to glow as if coming to life.

He added the sacred stones—onyx for strength, moonstone for vision, moss agate for healing, and jasper for courage—each placed at a cardinal point around the circle. The air grew heavy, electric, charged with a power that caused the hair on his arms to stand on end.

Next, the shaman lifted a bowl containing a thick, viscous brew made from rare herbs, the ground teeth of mountain lions, and rattlesnake venom. No shaman would dare consume it unless he sought to speak with the spirits or travel to the other side.

He drank it in one swift gulp, the bitter liquid burning his throat and sending fire into his veins. His vision blurred, and the cave seemed to twist and pulse as the potion took hold.

With the obsidian knife in hand, Kinetitah drew a deep cut across his palm, allowing his blood to spill into the circle. The pain was sharp, but he welcomed it; it anchored him, binding his spirit to the earth as his mind drifted into another realm.

He chanted louder, his voice echoing off the walls, his words a dark symphony that called upon ancient gods and restless souls. He plunged the knife into the ground, burying it to the hilt as a final act of defiance. The world around him trembled, producing a low rumble that grew steadily stronger until the cave shook violently. Rocks fell from the ceiling, crashing around him, but Kinetitah did not flinch.

A flash of light materialized to his right. It was a campfire. Next to the campfire sat his sister and niece. They two bore no emotions. Suddenly, deep gashes and cuts appeared all over their bodies. An unseen attacker was slashing and chopping at them. The two screamed in pain—terror-driven bellows of torment. Kinetitah was furious but helpless. His rage was boundless.

Then it began. The shaman's body convulsed, muscles tightening and bones cracking as if his very form was being torn apart and rebuilt. His skin bubbled and twisted, darkening and hardening into a scaly armor that shimmered like the hide of a serpent. His arms elongated, massive claws emerging where his hands had been. He doubled over, feeling his spine stretch and his chest expand as his heart pounded wildly. The owl skull amulet fused into his forehead, its red eyes glowing with a haunting light that pierced through the darkness.

Kinetitah roared in agony as his face contorted, his jaw elongating lined with rows of sharp, jagged teeth. His eyes, once brown, now blazed red, shimmering like embers in the night. He grew, towering over the fire, his head nearly scraping the cave ceiling. His breath came out in steaming puffs, hot and fetid, reeking of decay and death.

He was no longer human—he was a beast, a monster born of vengeance, forged in the fires of loss and rage. He stood on hind legs, his new form a grotesque blend of man, animal, and spirit, his claws digging into the earth as if to anchor himself to this world.

Kinetitah let out a guttural howl that reverberated through the cave, an ancient, vengeful, and unstoppable echo. He could feel the power coursing through him, the bear's strength, the owl's sight, and the wolf's savagery.

He stepped out of the cavern's mouth and into the night, his massive frame blending into the shadows. The forest fell silent at his presence; even the wind seemed to hold its breath. Then he roared. It was the most unearthly sound imaginable. As the roar resonated through the woods, Kinetitah, or whatever he became, vanished into thin air.

CHAPTER 5

The Return of Mad River Billy

February 26th, 1870

For the first nine years following the massacre, Mad River Billy's threats seemed hollow. There were no sightings, no stories of his whereabouts, and no retribution from the surviving Wiyot. The settlers began to believe he was either dead or had simply disappeared, taking his curse with him.

But on the tenth anniversary of the massacre, the eerie calm was shattered. People vanished. And among the missing was Mary Hurley, Timothy Hurley's eleven-year-old daughter.

Mary had been swimming with other children at a local spring when she wandered off searching for wildflowers. Moments after she disappeared into the foliage, a scream pierced the air. The other children ran from the water and searched for their friend, shouting her name and begging Mary to come out—but Mary was nowhere to be found.

Tommy Holsten, one of the boys at the spring, sprinted to the Hurley house, breathless and pale. "Mary's gone!" he blurted, his voice shaking.

Timothy Hurley grabbed the boy by the shoulders. "Gone where, Tommy? What happened?"

"She screamed!" Tommy cried. "She went into the woods, and then we heard her scream. I—I saw something."

Hurley's grip tightened. "What did you see? Speak clearly, boy!"

Tommy hesitated, glancing at the other children who had followed him. Finally, he whispered, "An Indian. He had feathers on his head, and he was running away through the woods."

"Mad River Billy," muttered Arnie Johnson, who'd been at the Hurley home.

"No," Hurley said sharply, shaking his head. "That's impossible. Billy disappeared years ago. There were rumors he fell off a cliff. It's not him."

"It has to be him. No one else would do such a thing," Johnson insisted, his face pale. "You remember what he said, Tim. He swore he'd come for us and our children. He said he'd return every ten years. Well, here we are."

Hurley's skepticism faltered as he looked at his son Jacob, who stood pale and silent. "Do you think it's Billy?" Hurley asked.

Jacob nodded, his voice barely audible. "It's him, Pa. It must be."

Jacob's father remained skeptical. "Listen. It's been ten years since he disappeared. It makes no sense. There were rumors that he died. Fell off a cliff or something. No, it seems impossible it could be him after all these years."

"Who else could it be? He said he'd avenge the massacre. He promised to get us and our kids, remember? He said he'd be back every ten years. And, by God, it's been ten years—to the day," Johnson said.

Trying to seek any other reasonable explanation, Timothy offered, "How about those two killings up north? The miners? Maybe their killers came here."

"Dad, those killings were fifty miles away. And I heard they were defending themselves from some claim jumpers. No, that doesn't make sense," Jacob interjected.

After a moment of thought, Jacob's father made his decision. "Okay. Arm yourselves and gather supplies. I'll get Fred and Donny Blanton, Ezra Taylor, Stovepipe, and my brother Nort. We'll meet back in an hour. Bring enough provisions for two to three days. Now go."

Two hours later, the search party assembled at the spring. Paul Peterson, known as 'Stovepipe,' for always wearing a stovepipe hat, brought his bloodhound, Dog. Hurley gave the hound Mary's nightdress to sniff. Dog breathed in her scent. He began snuffling around the ground, sounding like a miniature steam engine. Suddenly, the bloodhound let out a mournful bay before racing into the woods.

"He's on her scent! Damned if he isn't," Stovepipe announced, his Scottish brogue thick with hope.

The men chased after the hound, ever vigilant for any sign of the girl. But they followed for several miles without spotting Mary or Billy: no footprints, broken branches, or clues of any kind. Jacob, ahead of the older, slower searchers, was beginning to doubt the bloodhound's direction. He was leading them toward a part of the coast where no humans lived.

After an hour of pursuit, Dog came to a skidding halt, running in circles and sniffing frantically. Hackles raised; the hound finally found the first real clue: a sliver of Mary's dress snagged on a black elderberry bush. As the men caught up, Jacob held up the scrap of cloth.

"Billy's got her. The son of a bitch has her, I know it. Come on, we gotta catch up before it's too late. Stovepipe, get that damn mutt of yours going again," Mary's father pleaded.

"Come on, Dog, find Mary—now!" Stovepipe shouted. The dog took off again, ears flapping wildly as he sprinted away. The hunt continued for hours, and the men marveled at how the kidnapper managed to stay ahead while carrying a sixty-pound child.

The terrain rose sharply as they neared the coast. Stovepipe estimated they had climbed fifteen hundred to two thousand feet during the ascent. The steepness slowed the older men until their pace became a strained walk. Jacob, his youth still in play, pushed on.

A few minutes later, a woeful howl from Dog echoed through the woods, loud and urgent. Then, a gunshot rang out. And then another.

"Jacob!" Timothy Hurley yelled. "We're coming!" Moments later, the hunters rounded a bend and found Jacob and Dog standing in a small clearing.

"What happened? Did you see Mary?" Hurley asked, panting. "What were you shooting at?"

"When I got here, Dog was staring into those trees," Jacob gasped, pointing. "But he wouldn't go any further. I tried to push him on, but he was frozen and wouldn't budge. Then, a man stepped out from that dark patch of trees. I'm not sure if it was Billy, but it was an Indian," Jacob explained.

"Was Mary with him? Is she okay?"

"I didn't see Mary. But I didn't want him to get away, so I shot at him twice. Funny thing, though—he didn't go down or even stumble. I'm sure I hit him," Jacob said, removing his hat and wiping the sweat from his brow.

"Where is he now?" his father asked.

"He just turned like the shots were nothing and walked back into the woods."

"Let's get in there and find him," Hurley ordered. The group nodded, checked their weapons, and started toward the trees. And that's when it happened.

The earth began to convulse and shake. A violent earthquake, a monstrous echo of the one in 1700, erupted beneath the men. Panic swept over the hunters as they struggled to stay upright. The ground lurched and jolted like a bucking bronco. Branches fell like deadly artillery, and the men threw themselves into desperate dodges.

Jacob Hurley, disarmed and disoriented, fought for footing. His efforts were fruitless as he lost his balance, and his face slammed into the moist earth. A branch thick as his arm crashed onto his back, knocking the wind from his lungs.

Gasping, he clawed at the ground, struggling for breath as if drowning.

The forest roared, trees splintering as if the world itself were ending.

Then, as abruptly as it had begun, the shaking stopped. An eerie stillness settled over the woods, broken only by the faint rustle of falling leaves and broken twigs. The men lay scattered, dazed, their curses and prayers mingling with the echoes of destruction.

Timothy Hurley staggered to his feet, his desperation propelling him toward his injured son. "Jacob, son, are you okay? Answer me!"

Jacob's reply was weak, his words strained and pained. "I think so, Pa… just got the wind knocked out of me. My back hurts a little, but I don't think anything's broken."

"Let me take a look."

Timothy examined the tear in Jacob's shirt, where blood had soaked through. He moved the ripped cloth aside, revealing a nasty gash on the boy's back. "We'll need to patch this up," he said.

The rest of the group assessed their injuries—mostly minor compared to the destruction all around. They were thankful and prayed for their good fortune. Suddenly, all eyes turned to Jacob, who was pointing toward the woods with a trembling hand.

"Look!" he gasped, terror lending strength to his voice. "The Indian—and Mary!"

The men scrambled around for their weapons. Ezra, screaming like a banshee, sprinted toward the man with the same adrenaline-fueled fury he'd shown during the Wiyot massacre. His face twisted in rage as he charged forward, oblivious to everything but his desire to kill Mad River Billy and save Mary.

But twenty paces from his target, Ezra's vengeful sprint ended as the earth yawned before him—a massive chasm, a gash torn by the quake's wrath, blocking his path. His eyes widened, not with battle fury but sheer terror, as his momentum hurdled him over the edge.

"Stop!" Timothy Hurley yelled, throwing his arms out to halt the others. The men skidded to a stop, narrowly avoiding the same fate as Ezra. The men looked down at the mangled body of their friend. Their rage intensified.

Hurley's chest heaved as he looked across the chasm at the figure holding his daughter's limp body. His pulse pounded in his ears, drowning out any thought of whether Mary was alive. Vengeance consumed him—Mad Billy or not, this man would pay.

"Give me back my daughter, or I will shoot you," Hurley threatened, rifle aimed. The Indian, stoic and still, released the girl. She fell, lifeless, until—a faint twitch.

"She's alive! Mary just moved. MARY, CAN YOU HEAR ME?" Jacob shouted. But only silence answered, heavy and more haunting than any scream.

"Is it you? Are you Mad River Billy?" Timothy's voice wavered, tinged with desperation. "Spare your life. Just give me my child."

The man's gaze held steady, a deep well of hatred and sorrow. "When you return the slain of the Wiyot."

Hurley's eyes darted toward the others, all participants in the raid on Indian Island, and said feebly, "They're all dead. How can we give them back to you?"

"You should have thought of that before you butchered the innocent. Little boys and girls, like the one lying helpless at my feet, were hacked and slashed to death, some beyond recognition. And then you burned them along with everything survivors needed to survive. For your actions, you must pay the supreme penalty.

"Hurley, Blanton, Johnson, Taylor, Peterson—today and for years to come, you and many others will feel the wrath of Wiyot revenge. You, your children, and their children will suffer as we have."

"Father, should I scout for a way to get to the other side?" Jacob asked.

"Yes, and hurry. You and Arnie head that way. Stovepipe, you take Dog, and you and the Blantons go the other way," the elder Hurley ordered, pointing north and south. "Nort and I will stay here and make sure he doesn't try to leave." Turning back to the Indian, he added, "We will find a way to get to you. And when we do, our judgment will be delivered—not yours." As the two scouting parties prepared to depart, Stovepipe recoiled, his face contorting in disgust.

"Gods above, what is that stench? Something reeks of death."

"Hell, I ain't never smelled nothing that bad, dead or alive," Fred Blanton choked.

Johnson, Ezra Taylor's closest neighbor from town, had been standing at the edge of the gorge, staring down at his friend's mangled body. Ignoring the odor, Johnson said, "We gotta kill this bastard—now." He raised his rifle, took careful aim, and then, as his eyes widened in disbelief, he mouthed silently, "Oh, my God..."

CHAPTER 6

The Curse Awakens

In an unimaginable scene, Mad River Billy began to transform. His body expanded and morphed as if inflated by an invisible force. His arms, legs, and torso bulged grotesquely, skin stretching and tearing with sickening cracks as though his very being rebelled against nature. His swelling form tore through his buckskin clothes like paper, and his feathered headdress snapped and fell to the damp soil.

Johnson's voice broke through the eerie silence, raw and filled with dread. "What monstrosity is this?"

Stovepipe's bloodhound whimpered in terror before turning tail and disappearing into the shadows. "It's Satan. He's come to seek revenge for the wrongs we did," Stovepipe said, his voice trembling under the weight of their sins.

"God forgive us, Billy. Please, have mercy," Donny Blanton begged as he crumpled to his knees.

The being, no longer human, didn't answer; it only continued to change into something nature had never imagined. Where Mad River Billy's hands had been, there were now claws with razor-sharp talons. His human ears gave way to writhing, snake-like appendages. His eyes, once black as coal, had expanded to the size of saucers, glowing ember red.

Scales, some as large as panhandling tins, jutted from his body. And his mouth was now filled with rows of jagged, shark-like teeth. Where a man once stood, a grotesque, hideous fifteen-foot beast now towered above them.

Then, as if by magic, a woman and small child appeared at the monster's side. Cuts and gouges savaged their bodies, and their hair was scorched away.

As if the sight alone wasn't enough to paralyze them with fear, the creature bellowed—a roar so chilling, it turned their blood and nerves to ice. The Blantons, overcome with terror, fled into the woods, screaming hysterically. Once a paragon of strength, Norton Hurley collapsed, sobbing like a child.

Jacob and Timothy Hurley clung to each other. "Father," Jacob wept, "what shall we do? How can we save Mary from such a creature?"

Upon hearing his daughter's name, Timothy Hurley's resolve reignited. He gently pushed Jacob aside and shouldered his rifle. At this range, and given the creature's enormous size, he couldn't miss. Shaking like a leaf and with tears in his eyes, Hurley took aim. The beast, its mocking gaze fixed on him, stood unmoved.

Hurley's shot rang out, slicing through the air with deadly accuracy. Yet, as if defying the laws of nature, the bullet glanced off the creature's scales, ricocheting harmlessly into the forest.

Lowering its head to inspect the spot where the bullet hit, the creature chuffed, a sound that was almost like laughter. It growled in a gravelly voice that seemed to pierce Hurley's very soul, "A decade has passed since you committed your atrocity.

Today, my harvest begins—and every ten years from now, I will take a life from each of your families. And though I could devour each of you now, I need you to suffer with each loss.

"Do not worry. Your day will soon come. And know this: there is no place on earth you can hide from my reach. And on the centennial of your crime, the very last of your lineage will end with me devouring the last of your blood as restitution. Only then shall the spirits of the Wiyot find peace."

With its curse cast and with the woman and child in tow, the monstrous entity retreated into the forest's shadows, Mary limp in its grasp, leaving behind a silence that echoed with despair.

"What did it mean? It took one from each of us," Norton Hurley begged, his voice quivering. His brother could only look at him and shake his head in confusion. "My God, Timothy. Does that mean—?"

"And who were the woman and child?" Jacob muttered.

There was a moment of silence that was deafening. And then the elder Hurley muttered, "Could it be? No, they were dead when we left the village. I know, I'm the one who, well, you know."

"Timothy, could that have been Billy's sister and niece? Oh my God. Satan has surely unleashed his hell on us. We are doomed," Johnson sobbed.

When Mary's search party returned home, Timothy Hurley's wife, looking years older than her age, broke down upon learning her daughter was dead. She never recovered from the loss and died heartbroken two years later.

The other men discovered that one person from each of their families had died under mysterious circumstances. Some were spouses, others were children, two were elderly parents.

As the days passed, the shadow of the beast's curse became a gruesome reality—one by one, the households of those involved in the massacre began to fall, the prophecy unfolding with ruthless precision. Dozens of people of all ages had perished.

CHAPTER 7

The Reckoning

February 20th, 1880

Frank Tyson's Hunting Lodge

Humboldt County, CA

Arnie Johnson's voice trembled with uncertainty. "Tim, for God's sake, what are we doing here? We have no idea where this crazy Indian might be. And even if we find him, the last time we tried to kill the bastard, things didn't turn out so well. I can't believe you talked us into coming."

"Listen, we've been searching for Billy for a decade and haven't found a single sign of him. But if he's true to his word about showing up every ten years, then the bastard is coming for us—or worse, one of our family members. We can't let that happen again, can we?" Timothy Hurley demanded.

"If all accounts are correct, he's already killed dozens, including my Mary, Nort's son Sean, and what about your sister, Arnie? She went to visit a friend and never came home. Don, Fred, how about you two? Want anyone else in your family to disappear? And how about all the rest of the families involved in that godforsaken day? All missing someone. And then there's Ezra's body—or what's left of it—sitting at the bottom of that damn ravine."

There was silence for several heartbeats, and then Fred Blanton said, "Maybe Billy's gone for good, or maybe his threat to come after us every ten years wasn't real. But it's been twenty years since we did what we did, and ten years since my son Joseph…you know. And I, for one, do not want to take a chance. I say let's kill that bastard."

"I hear what you're saying, but I think Arnie's got a point. I feel like the odds are stacked heavily in that thing's favor. We need to get more help," Frank Tyson said.

Hurley's cynicism was palpable. "Sure, let's call the whole town to arms against an enemy that time forgot, an apparition that becomes flesh but once in a blue moon. They'd say we were insane. Besides, the blame for the massacre would come up all over again."

Hurley paused, then added with conviction, "Listen, we agreed Billy must die before another transformation occurs. But if we can't kill him for some reason, and we face that monstrosity again, I've got this." From a case he carried, Hurley pulled out a Nitro Express rifle, one of the most powerful guns ever built. "I don't care what it's made of—this baby will drill right through it."

"Wow, Tim, where'd you get that?" Tyson asked.

"It's on loan from Ernie Rodriguez. He got it from his father a few years ago. The two went grizzly hunting in Alaska, and Ernie said it only took one shot to take down a five hundred-pounder. Made a hole so big you could bury your fist in it. Yep, this is the mother of all guns."

Deacon's hand twitched with eagerness. "I bet that thing could kill an elephant. Let me fire it."

"I can't do it, Deak. Ammo is scarce, and our purpose is singular—kill that monster," Hurley said, turning to the rest of the men. "This is it. We are the line between the past and our future. We hunt at dawn—for vengeance, peace, and the end of a curse that has shadowed us for too long. Not one other person will die because of what we did. Now, get some sleep; we go to war against the demon at sunrise."

"I hope it also kills the demons I've been carrying around with me for twenty years," David Tucker said sorrowfully.

The fire crackled as they settled into a silence that spoke louder than any words.

****

"Almost three days and no sign of him," Tucker's voice cracked as he wiped a weary hand across his brow. He looked at a desolate Hurley and said, "Tim, we're down to the bare bones of our food supply. We'll have to go back if we don't find Billy soon. Arnie's wife is due to give birth any day now, and he's getting antsy about going home."

Hurley's gaze was distant, but his words carried quiet determination. "I know, and it gnaws at me. That accursed ravine stands between us and success. I'm sure of it—he's there, lurking. We've scoured the earth everywhere else."

"You know, we found that spot this morning, and it's only about twenty-five feet wide. We could erect a makeshift bridge if we cut down two sturdy pines and tied them together. It'd only take us an hour or so. What do you think?" Tucker offered.

"Might be our only option," Hurley said, his voice heavy with the gravity of their situation. He thought for a moment, then spat, "Damn it! Tomorrow marks twenty years to the day. We must find this son-of-a-bitch and kill him. Deak, Frank, grab your axes."

Forty-five minutes later, the group stood poised, the felled trees bound and braced. "Okay, let's stand these up, and once we get them steady and lined up, we'll drop them down to land on the other side. Ready?" Hurley asked the others. They all nodded resolutely. "Let's lift them."

Before the men could heft the trees, a cry pierced their focus. "Dad! Dad, it's me—Jacob!" The voice echoed.

"Jacob? Jacob, is that you, boy?" Tim Hurley shouted.

"Yeah. I'm coming in."

When Tim's son appeared, Hurley boomed, "Jacob, what part of 'you're not coming' didn't you understand? And why is Abe Junior with you?"

"Abe Junior came to the house this morning and asked me where you were. Said his ma needed his pa. I knew I couldn't let him come by himself. He'd never have found you. So, I brought him," Jacob explained.

When young Arnold's gaze met his father's, the urgency was unmistakable. "Pa, it's happening. Ma's in labor, and it's not going well. Doc Pritchett's with her, but he says you must come now."

"Tim, forgive me. I gotta go," Johnson said, gathering his gear.

"I can take Mr. Johnson's place, and he can return with Junior. You'll be one man down if I don't, and besides, I got as much right to be here as any other man. Billy killed my baby sister, and I want him dead," Jacob exclaimed.

"No. You're not staying. I'm not taking any chances of losing you, too. Plus, you have a new wife you need to think about and a baby of your own on the way. You're going with Mr. Johnson, and that's the end of it," Hurley said sternly. He looked away from Jacob and addressed Johnson. "Arnie, go to your wife and take my son with you. You make sure he goes all the way home. Do you hear?"

"You got it, Tim," Johnson agreed, then considered the others. "Kill Satan's bastard and get back safely. I'll be waiting," he finished and headed off.

Jacob regarded his dad with resentful eyes but knew better than to argue. He stomped his foot, turned, and raced after the Johnsons.

"Now we're just four," Deacon Howard mumbled.

"No matter," Hurley declared, steely-eyed as he led the way. "We'll find him, and we'll finish him."

As night's embrace tightened, Tyson's voice broke the silence. "Tim, we'll be stumbling around in pitch blackness soon. Shouldn't we wait till tomorrow when we'll have more light?"

"Fellas, tomorrow is the twenty-sixth. Maybe that doesn't mean a thing. But with each passing minute, we get closer to a deadline none of us want to face. I'll tell you what. Let's scout the area a bit longer to see if we can discover any signs of him. There are three trails here. One goes right, one left, and one heads toward the ocean. Let's pick one and search there. If we don't find anything, we'll return to camp and start again in the morning. Fair?"

"Yeah, I'm good with that. You guys?" Tyson responded. Tucker and Howard nodded in agreement.

"Okay. Let's go down the one heading toward the ocean. Follow me," Hurley said.

Thirty minutes later, the four found no evidence of any human presence. Frustration set in as they grew hungry and tired. "Let's head back," Hurley said. "We'll check the other two trails tomorrow."

"What if we don't find anything?" Tyson's question hung in the air like a specter.

"We give it one more night. If he remains a ghost, then perhaps his threats were nothing but the breath of a deranged madman," Hurley murmured. He said the words but didn't believe them. Billy was out here alright; he'd bet his life on it. And he'd come for them or their loved ones if they didn't find and kill him first.

"Boys, we've got some beef jerky and four potatoes for dinner tonight. Oh, and I think there are still two tomatoes from my garden. Besides that, there's nothing else to eat," Tucker, the group's cook, said as they ambled back to camp.

"And I still have some rye from Everett Jackson's still left over. I could use a drink. How about you guys?" Frank Tyson chimed in.

"Yeah, but we must keep our wits about us. So, we gotta go easy," Hurley cautioned.

"How much farther?" Tucker asked.

"If I remember correctly, we should come to the ravine after that next turn," Hurley answered. "Yep, there it is. Deak, light your torch so we can see better." Howard retrieved his flint and lit the torch. The four men crossed without issue.

Once on the other side, Frank squinted into the darkness. "What's that? Is there a fire in our camp?"

"Maybe Arnie came back," Tucker said, then paused. "Nah, that can't be. He wouldn't leave Evelyn so soon, would he?"

"If it's Jacob, I'm going to tan the hide off that boy. I don't care how old he is," Hurley said.

"Could it be Billy?" Howard asked. With those words, each man stopped dead in their tracks and readied his weapon. They moved closer and saw two figures asleep next to a small fire.

"Who the hell is that?" Tucker asked.

"I know this sounds crazy, but it looks like a woman and a child. Indians, I think," Hurley said. "Let's get a little closer. Deak, you and Frank go left, over by those bushes. Wait in hiding until we see what's going on." The two nodded and quietly made their way to the spot. "Come on, Dave. Let's see what this is all about."

"Hello, you two. What are you doing in here?" Hurley shouted, but the sleeping forms didn't move. "I said, what are you doing here? Who are you?"

The flames of the fire began to grow, rising several feet higher than when the four first arrived. Hurley took a small step back, bumping into Tucker.

"What the hell is going on?" Tucker said, his voice catching in his throat. Before Hurley could answer, a terrifying shriek filled the air.

Frank and Deacon didn't wait for Hurley's call; they raced back to where the two men stood.

"Christ, what was that?" Frank begged as they ran up. Then, another shriek, equally loud and horrifying.

"Look!" Deacon yelled. The sleeping figures began jostling, squirming and twisting like someone or something was manhandling them. Suddenly, wounds appeared on their arms, shoulders, faces, and hands, blood splattering from the cuts. It was as if invisible knives were viciously slashing them.

The women screamed in bone-chilling agony, their cries slicing through the night. The men stood frozen, paralyzed by the horror unfolding before their eyes.

"We have to do something," Tucker shouted.

"Do what? Who do we shoot? There's no one there," Hurley replied. He was right. No visible attackers could be seen. In stunned horror, they watched as the older woman's body shot up into a kneeling position. Her head jerked back, her hair snapping upright, and a deep slash opened across her neck. Blood gushed from the wound, pouring down her chest in torrents.

"My God, it's them," Tim Hurley gasped. The site a memory of his own actions.

But the horror only deepened. As if the fire itself had a murderous intent, flames leaped onto the Indians, igniting their clothes and hair. Their wails of agony filled the air as their skin began to melt under the searing heat.

Then, as unexpectedly as the nightmare began, the entire scene vanished, plunging the campsite into total darkness.

"I can't see a thing," Howard said.

"Me neither," Tyson shouted.

"Deacon. Where's your damn torch?" Hurley demanded.

"I dropped it when I heard that scream—scared the hell out of me. When I looked down, the flame was out, so I left it there," Hurley said, his voice panicked.

"Where did the women go? And how could there be a fire one second and then gone the next? I don't see a burning coal or ember. You'd at least see a red glow, wouldn't you?" Tucker pleaded.

"Yes. I mean, I think," Hurley replied. Then a red glow did appear—but not on the ground where the fire had been. It was a dozen feet up in the trees, two glowing embers, round and seemingly moving together, dancing in the darkness. "You have come," a deep, raspy voice said. "I knew you would, and I have been waiting. Now I can keep my word as promised."

"Billy. Is that you?" Tucker stammered.

"I am Puchúri-ghúrru. I am Ki-ne-ti-tah. Or, if you prefer, I am the one you call Billy."

"Are you the one who killed my daughter?" Hurley asked.

"You killed your daughter, Timothy Hurley. Her fate was sealed the moment your people slaughtered the Wiyot. By killing the innocent, you cursed your children, yourselves, and, one day, every living member of your families. I warned you. And now, none of you will leave this place. I will feed on your souls as the next payment for your atrocities."

"Not if I can help it!" Hurley shouted, firing the Nitro Express. The blast roared, and a huge flame shot from its barrel.

"Did you get him?" Howard asked, desperation in his voice.

"I'm certain I did. He was right in front of us. I couldn't have missed. We need some light. Somebody find that torch!"

Suddenly, a bloodcurdling scream erupted to Hurley's left. "Was… was that Dave screaming?" Hurley choked out. "Dave! Dave, are you okay?" Before any answer could come, another horrifying shriek rang out, this time to Hurley's right. "What the hell is going on? Deak? Dave? Frank? Where are you guys?" A third scream, unmistakably Frank Tyson, exploded into the evening air, more desperate and disturbing than the first two.

Hurley fumbled for another shell for the rifle, but it slipped from his grasp and fell to the ground. He dropped to his knees and began searching. His hand landed on something wet and slimy. After a moment, he realized it was an arm—but the limb wasn't attached to a body.

"Jesus, Joseph, and Mary," Hurley cried. At that moment, a fire ignited in front of him, illuminating the woods. It also revealed his companions—or what was left of them. They had been torn apart; their limbs scattered around the camp. Hurley was mortified and started to weep.

A voice filled with malice called out from beyond the light, "Once, you were the vanquishers. Tonight, it is you who will be vanquished."

Hurley heard bushes rustling and heavy footsteps thudding through the darkness. He scrambled around trying to find the gun ammo he'd dropped. And then he found the shell. He picked it up and raised his gun to load it. Standing in front of him was a beast from hell, towering at least fifteen feet tall.

Hurley's fingers dropped the ammo.

The flickering flames distorted its features, making it beyond terrifying, but Hurley could see the worst. A gigantic, misshapen head with two saucer-sized, glowing red eyes, snakelike figures sprouting from its head, and rows of jagged, razor-sharp teeth.

The creature glowered at Hurley. "Timothy Hurley. Know that you are about to die in a manner befitting the atrocities you and these men have committed. As I consume your body and soul, remember, every member of your family will eventually die by my hands. Carry that with you to your grave." The creature's mouth began to open, the gaping orifice growing wider and wider until all Hurley could see were teeth...

CHAPTER 8

Jacob Part 2

February 25th, 1910

"Do you see it? To the right of that stump. They blend in well, but it's there," Jacob Hurley said, his voice low and steady as he crouched behind thick brush.

Timmy Hurley, fourteen and eager to prove himself, squinted into the undergrowth. His wiry frame was taut with concentration. "I don't. I don't see it, Pa." He paused, scanning the shadows. Then, his voice quickened with excitement. "Wait—it moved! There it is!"

"Shush," Jacob hissed, holding up a hand. "You have to keep your voice down. You don't want to spook it." He leaned in closer, his face grim and lined with years of hard living. "This is one of the most ferocious animals alive. If it attacks, it won't just hurt you—it'll kill you. Those tusks can rip your guts out."

Timmy's excitement faltered, replaced by a flicker of fear. He whispered, "Gee, Pa, sorry." He adjusted his grip on the rifle slung over his shoulder. "Okay… what do we do?"

Jacob's expression softened. "We're gonna move real quiet over there, to the right of where it's hiding. Once we're in position, we'll wait for it to come out. Then you can take the shot."

"You mean it?" Timmy's face lit up with pride. "I've never shot a boar before. Thanks, Pa."

Jacob nodded, his lips twitching into a faint smile. "Grandpa would be proud. Now, stay low and follow me."

Father and son slid to the right, their movements deliberate and noiseless. The forest was alive with its usual hum—leaves rustling in the breeze, birds chittering faintly—but something caught Timmy's eye. A flicker of movement to his left. Was that an Indian? No, not out here, Timmy reasoned. But as they crept along the well-worn animal trail, Timmy couldn't shake the feeling that someone or something was out there.

"Pa?"

"Shh." Jacob didn't look back.

"But, Pa, I saw something over there. In the woods."

Jacob stopped. He turned, his expression narrowing. "What? Where? Another boar?"

"No." Timmy hesitated, his tone dropping. "I think it was… it might've been an Indian. Are Indians bad? Could they hurt us? I heard people saying they want to hurt folks like us."

Jacob's jaw tightened. He scanned the tree line, raising his rifle slightly. "Never mind that," he said, his tone hard. "Where did you see him?"

Timmy pointed toward the trees, but there was nothing—just empty woods.

Jacob stared for a moment longer, then turned back to Timmy, his expression grim. "Okay, we're leaving," he said abruptly. "Don't ask me why. Just follow me and stay close."

"But Pa—"

And then it happened.

A roar tore through the forest, so loud and guttural that it seemed to shake the ground beneath their feet. Both father and son screamed in fright.

"Run!" Jacob bellowed, grabbing Timmy by the arm and shoving him forward. "Don't stop! No matter what you hear or see, you keep going. If anything happens to me, you get home. You got me? Get home!"

"You're scaring me, Pa!" Timmy cried, his voice breaking. "What's going on?"

"Just stay—" Jacob's words were cut short by a thunderous crash ahead. The sound was deafening like a tree being ripped from the earth. Jacob's eyes widened in panic, and without thinking, he veered sharply to the left, dragging Timmy along into the heavy brush.

The two clawed through thorns and undergrowth, branches slapping their faces and snagging their clothes. Timmy could feel the sting of cuts on his arms and cheeks, warm blood trickling down his neck.

"What is it? What's after us?" Timmy shouted.

"Don't look back! Stay with me!" Jacob's words came out raw. He was scared too, terrified because he knew what was out there and what it meant to do.

They stumbled onto a worn path that wound through the trees. Jacob grabbed Timmy's hand and ran as fast as he could, the boy struggling to keep up. The growling roar followed them, closer now, a sound so unnatural it made the hair on the back of Timmy's neck stand on end.

After what felt like an eternity, Jacob slowed, chest heaving as he glanced back. The forest was still. No sign or sound of anything following.

"Okay," Jacob panted. "I think we lost it."

Timmy dropped to his knees, clutching his sides as he gasped for breath. "Lost what?" he begged, his eyes wide with terror. "What was that thing?"

Jacob didn't answer. His face was pale, his eyes distant.

"Pa?" Timmy pressed. "You have to tell me! You're acting like... like it's not just an animal. Was it—was it the curse?"

Jacob froze. The word hung in the air like a blade, sharp and heavy. For a moment, all Timmy could hear was the rustle of leaves, the forest whispering around them. The sounds should have been comforting, but they weren't.

"Don't talk about that," Jacob warned, his voice low and tense. "Not here. Not ever."

"But—"

"Enough!" Jacob snapped. Timmy flinched, and the reaction seemed to soften his father's expression. He knelt, placing a steadying hand on Timmy's shoulder. "I'll explain when we're safe," he said, his tone quieter now. "Not here. Not where it can hear us."

"Where *what* can hear us?" Timmy asked, his voice shaking.

Jacob didn't answer. He stood, pulling Timmy to his feet. "Like I said. I'll tell you when we're safe. Let's move."

The two pressed on, their pace brisk but cautious. Jacob kept one hand on his rifle his knuckles white against the stock. Timmy followed close, his heart racing, his mind spinning with questions he was warned not to ask.

As time passed, the forest grew darker, the shadows longer, until it felt like they were walking through a tunnel of black. The sounds of the woods—birds, insects, the rustle of leaves—faded, replaced by a heavy, oppressive silence.

And then a low, guttural growl rolled through the trees like distant thunder. It was deeper than the roar from before, more deliberate, more menacing.

Jacob stopped dead and held up a hand to signal Timmy to do the same.

"Pa…" Timmy whispered, clutching his father's sleeve.

"Quiet," Jacob breathed, his eyes scanning the underbrush. "He's close. I can feel his presence."

Something moved to their left.

Jacob spun, raising his rifle with trembling hands. Two women, one an adult and one a child, were sitting beside a small campfire—neither they nor the fire were there seconds before. The two were in a desperate hug as if scared to death from some unseen menace. But the elder Hurley knew immediately who they were. Their image had been forever etched in his mind. Twenty years ago, they had been there when his sister Mary was taken. And just like then, he knew this was no coincidence.

"You won't have my son!" Jacob roared, leveling his shotgun at the two figures. But when he fired, the steel pellets passed through them as if they weren't there.

Jacob began to reload, and that's when the women started screaming. The sound was inhuman, a wail of pain and fury that pierced the air like a thousand knives. Timmy clapped his hands over his ears, but it didn't block the horror of their cries.

As if the moment couldn't have been worse, slashes appeared on the women. Huge gashes erupting across their heads, faces, arms, and torsos. Horrifying wounds that spewed copious amounts of gory red blood. Timmy screamed and covered his eyes. And it was a good thing as the next shocking sight was when the flames from the fire leaped onto the women. Their hair evaporated, and their skin began to sizzle and peel away.

"NO, NO, NO! Not again. Timmy, run!" Jacob yelled at his son. But the boy clung to his father like a starving leech.

Jacob pulled the boy's arms away, grabbed him by the hand, and raced away. Where he was going, he had no clue. All he knew was that he needed to get as far away from those women as possible. Because what was sure to appear next would be the last thing he or his son would ever see. He was certain of that.

The two ran until Timmy's legs could go no further. "Pa, I can't go on," Timmy pleaded.

Jacob stopped and turned to his boy. "Son, I know you're tired and scared. But you must be brave. I need you to do that. Can you? Can you be brave for your Pa?"

The boy's sobs had subsided, but he was still clearly petrified. "I'll try," Timmy said, with little conviction in his tone.

"Good. I knew you would. Now. We need to figure out where we are so we can get home. We won't be able to see a thing soon, so we have to find a trail out of here or a place to hide for the night.

Jacob pulled out a compass from his pants pocket. He held it up and watched the dial move until it stopped due north. That direction was behind him and slightly to the east.

"Okay, we need to go this way to find our way out of here. But I don't want to go on a direct path because it might bring us back to where those women were. So, let's go west for a while and then head south along the coastline. We'll travel that way until we reach Sutter's Point. From there even you know the way home. Sound good?"

"Sure Pa. If you say so," Timmy said with a nod.

"Great. Okay, follow me and stay close. You could get lost very easily out here, so let's not get separated. Let's go," Jacob said as he patted his son on the shoulder.

The two walked for about forty-five minutes when they followed a turn in the path that led to a small clearing. Jacob stopped dead. "No. This can't be. No way we're this far north," he said as he grabbed his son by the arm.

"Where are we, Pa?" Timmy asked, concern matching his father's.

In front of the two was the ravine surrounding the remains of Orca. Jacob couldn't understand how they could have come this far. It made no sense.

"This is a bad place, Timmy. We must get out of here," Jacob said. As he turned to go, an Indian was standing there…it was Mad River Billy.

"Your time has come, you and your son," Billy said. And then he began to change.

CHAPTER 9

The Edge of Oblivion

February 23rd, 1940
Ferndale, Northern California

Peter Blanton worked for Taylor Benson Products of San Francisco for the better part of three years. He started in the warehouse as a picker while learning to drive the delivery rigs on weekends.

In time, after Mr. Benson put him through rigorous tests, Peter became the youngest driver on the five-person delivery team—the youngest driver ever for Benson. Unfortunately, as with all new drivers, Blanton received the company's worst delivery region: up and through King Range, California.

The early going was rough, but though he'd only been working his territory a few months, he felt confident as he maneuvered the Harvester around the area's narrow roads. Yes, Peter believed he was a pretty good trucker. However, as his grandmother used to say, "Peter, my boy, shine where you can shine." And boy did he radiate with the ladies.

After finishing his Ferndale deliveries, Peter checked into the local Land's End Motel. While sitting in the motel's small cafe, he spotted a poster promoting the Humboldt County Fair, which had started the day before and would end that weekend. Thinking the carnival would be a welcome respite from his usual stay in town, Peter showered, splashed on some

56

Old Spice, applied a dab of Brylcreem to his hair, and headed toward the fair.

After waiting in line, Peter leaned down to offer his fifteen cents entry fee to the attendant in the ticket booth. What he saw through the window shook him, causing him to whistle involuntarily. Selling the tickets was Ida Lynn Dillon. The girl's wholesome beauty took his breath away.

With auburn hair flowing in a ponytail, a round, cherubic face dusted with freckles, and bright green eyes that sparkled like emeralds, Dillon captivated Peter. He ogled her petite but curvy figure, his gaze unwavering as she fidgeted with a bulky roll of red tickets.

They stared at each other for several long moments. Peter's expression radiated the raw intensity of youthful lust, while Ida Lynn's eyes held a spark of intrigue.

The ticket attendant knew every boy in Ferndale, and this wasn't one of them. Here stood someone who might provide options and possibilities for Ida Lynn—unlike the locals who seemed destined to stay trapped in the town forever. That was a picture she promised herself she would never paint—no matter what. This boy was cute, which was a bonus. But she fancied him for reasons he would never guess.

"Hey, Ace, are you going in or just gonna stand there and stare at me?" Ida Lynn said curtly.

"Oh, yeah. I'm buying," Peter said, embarrassed. He slid his money to her. As he took the ticket, he brushed his hand along Ida Lynn's, causing a small squeak to escape her lips and a bright blush to spread across her cheeks. Sensing his chance, Peter grinned. "You're quite the cookie, you know that?"

The statement triggered a giggle from Ida Lynn and a bashful turn of her head.

"What time do you finish here?" He asked.

"Why do you care?" she replied, shooting him a bold glare.

"Well, I'm not from here, and I could sure use someone's help gettin' through your fair."

"Hah," she said with a disbelieving laugh. "You don't need me to show you around. This fair's not that big."

"Well, maybe, but… heck, I'd like you to show me all the same," Peter said with an "aw shucks" charm.

"I don't know," the girl hesitated, trying not to reveal her genuine enthusiasm. "Besides, I don't get off till seven p.m., almost three hours from now. You'll have time to go through the fair five times by then," Ida Lynn said. "Now, move along, Ace. I got people waiting to get in!"

The lanky, good-natured boy spun around to see a life size version of Brutus from the Popeye comics staring down at him. Peter turned back to Ida Lynn, detecting an annoyed expression. Sighing, he dropped his head in dejection and walked away.

After a few steps, Peter's smile reemerged. Always resolute, he'd never given up on a girl in his life, and he wasn't about to start now. His grin widened.

In the ticket booth, a similar grin creased Ida Lynn's face, one that seemed almost cunning. He'd be back; she counted on it.

Blanton returned several times during the late afternoon, displaying a beaming and hopeful smile, only to be playfully rebuffed by Ida Lynn. Though he began questioning his ability to win her over, Peter made sure he was standing by the back of the booth a few minutes before seven p.m., just in case.

The boy shuffled from foot to foot in anticipation. Right on time, a bubble-gum-chewing blond girl glided past him, went up to the ticket booth door, and opened it. Within seconds, Ida Lynn burst out and, without a word, grabbed the bewildered Blanton by the arm, dragging him toward the clanging carnival rides. Soon, they were enveloped in the mingled smells of cotton candy, fiddlesticks, and fried everything. He was in!

Although born in Waterloo, Iowa, Blanton's family traced its roots back to some of the original settlers in the Ferndale area. Waterloo had served him well enough, but a distant cousin wrote about the booming opportunities for young men in California. The cousin claimed there were more jobs than people, but more to the point for Peter, the women outnumbered the men three to one.

That was all Peter needed to hear. And now, though only a route driver for a short while, didn't he already have a sweetheart in almost every town he delivered to? And hadn't his wit, charm, and good looks ultimately won Ida Lynn over? Yeah, California was the place to be for Peter Blanton! Moving here had been a blessing.

Each time Ida Lynn squeezed his arm and flashed him a smile, Peter felt certain he'd charmed her into doing exactly what he wanted. But Ida Lynn had her own plans.

The girl had spent the first twelve years of her life on Chicago's bustling, fast-paced streets near Wrigley Field. Childhood friends filled her memories, as did neighborhood stores and food vendors who greeted her by name. She still could smell the rich aromas of those foods. Her father instilled in her a love for the Cubs—and an intense dislike for the White Sox. She missed everything about the city.

And now, here was this unwitting boy, her potential ticket back to Chicago—and she was going for it.

After Peter spent five cents each on two caramel apples, the pair strolled the fairgrounds, inseparable for nearly four hours. They rode a few rides, including the Ferris wheel, where Ida Lynn kept her hand on his leg, and Peter won her a Kewpie doll at the ball toss arcade. They visited the livestock expo, gawked at Burl Thomas' record 900-pound pig—the biggest in the fair's history—and watched the mule team and tractor races.

While walking through the poultry exhibit, Peter put his hand on the small of Ida Lynn's back, sending a rush of chills up and down her spine. Though her reasons for being with him were calculated and different, his touch still gave her a thrill.

By eleven p.m., when the fair was closing, Ida Lynn decided. She would seduce Peter Blanton with her charms, and he would be hooked. Then, on one of his future trips to Ferndale, she would convince him to take her somewhere with real people—maybe even back to Chicago.

Now twenty-two, Ida Lynn needed a life. To stay in Ferndale would be like a prison sentence. So, when Peter suggested she go with him to his motel room, she said yes, though she feigned reluctance. After all, she wasn't some khaki wacky!

****

Peter breathed in deeply, savoring his victorious night. He had spent an incredible evening with the enchanting small-town girl and had shined! The memory of Ida Lynn's insatiable desire caused him to chuckle with giddy delight. She had praised him, raving about his prowess and how wonderful he made her feel—pure heaven. God, he was good.

After getting his paperwork in order, Blanton checked his watch: 6:30 a.m. He turned the diesel engine starter switch one notch and waited for the glow plugs to heat before initiating the starter. The Harvester's motor roared to life, and the delighted driver was set to go.

California cities such as Petrolia, Shelter Cove, and Whitethorn sprouted up in some of California's roughest, most inhospitable terrain. Engineers had yet to find suitable roadway routes, so only smaller rigs with proper gearing could traverse the slithering coastal routes.

After Ferndale, only two stops remained on his schedule. Capetown would be a breeze. But after that, there was the ever strange town of Orca. He hated going there and often wished it would burn to the ground. Everything about the area and the town creeped him out.

He scanned his paperwork one last time, thought of Ida Lynn lying naked in the motel, smiled again, and shifted the truck into first gear. Turning out of the motel's parking lot, he geared up and headed down State Route 211 towards Mattole Road and Capetown.

Peter had finished the delivery at Capetown by 11:30 a.m. By 2 p.m., he was turning onto Mendocino Road from Mattole Road. This part of his trip from Capetown to Orca offered a rare straight stretch, about a mile long. Toward the end of Mattole, the road tilted down at a slight angle. At the bottom of the incline was the bridge spanning a deep ravine that encircled Orca.

After crossing the span, there would be a hard left turn through the forest, an uphill right, and then a sloping right. Fifty yards beyond that, the wooded area would end, and the town of Orca would come into view. The drive was tricky, and Peter struggled early on. But after repeated trips, he now glided through the landscape with ease.

Whistling "Wabash Cannonball," Blanton navigated this section of Mattole Road without incident. With only a few hundred feet left to the bridge and traveling at about thirty-five miles an hour, something strange caught his eye. The small wooden bridge, one he often feared wouldn't hold his rig, appeared to be moving. At first, Peter's mind struggled to comprehend what was happening.

What at first looked like a small sway of the upper part of the bridge intensified into a severe wobble. In reaction, Peter's right foot slammed on the brake while his left foot depressed the truck's clutch. His vehicle should have slowed and then stopped, but instead, the International Harvester began bouncing up and down, edging forward and down the slight drop toward the bridge.

To Blanton, it felt like being back on the tilting rodeo ride from the Humboldt County Fair, except this was no goofy carnival attraction. No, this was an earthquake.

Peter's face contorted in terror as he realized the bridge's movements were due to the violent tremor. He also understood that he couldn't allow any part of his vehicle to be on the bridge when it stopped. If the structure collapsed and the Harvester was on it when it did, he would face certain death.

With eyes wide with fear and tears streaming down his face, Peter realized this could be the end. He imagined the abyss swallowing him and his rig like a vast carnivorous beast devouring its prey. Then, things got worse. The timber constructed span, which had been swaying like a suspension bridge caught in a storm, vanished. It simply disappeared, leaving an open void.

By this surreal moment, the truck's front wheels sat less than ten feet from nothingness.

Though the craggy, rock-filled crevasse existed long before Peter started traveling there, he had never taken the time to gauge its depth. He often glanced into the gorge while driving across the bridge, but the distance never registered, as he really didn't want to know. The drop could have been a thousand feet—or more, and the thought scared the heck out of him.

Squeezing his eyes shut, he kept his feet on the brakes, praying the truck would stop before plunging into the ravine. And then it did. The quake, which lasted almost a full minute but felt like an eternity, finally ceased. When the shaking stopped, and the earth returned to stillness, his vehicle stopped, too.

Taking his first conscious breath in what seemed like ages, Peter opened his eyes. As he looked around and saw the utter destruction all around, he realized he had somehow escaped death. He began to laugh. It started as a small giggle, then grew into a chuckle, and soon, he was laughing hysterically.

"Holy shit!" he shouted, his neck taut and strained. "That was goddamn close! Holy shit!"

It took him a few moments to calm down and regain what little composure he had left. He'd never experienced the effects of an earthquake, though he knew they happened and had been warned about them before moving to California. As he looked around, Peter couldn't believe what he was seeing. The area resembled World War 2 battlefield pictures he'd seen in Life Magazine.

Dozens of trees of different types lay on the ground, their roots now out of the ground. Most of the larger Redwoods remained unscathed except for broken limbs and branches. However, one massive tree, easily ten feet in diameter, did collapse, toppling less than a car's length from where Peter sat. If it had fallen a few feet to the left, the enormous tree would have crushed him and the truck like an ant under a boot. "Holy mackerel. That was a miracle," Peter muttered, whistling at his good fortune in escaping certain death.

Blanton reached for the door handle to get out when he noticed movement on the other side of the ravine. Three people now stood on the opposite bank. But they weren't just people—they were Indians. A man dressed in full-length deerskin, wearing a war bonnet, his face painted, carrying a bow and a long knife. Beside him stood a woman and a small girl.

Peter wasn't sure what to do. He considered waving but decided that to be a foolish gesture. He then thought about getting out to see if the Indians needed help. But with the bridge gone, they were stranded.

The male Indian made a series of gestures, waving his arms in different directions before raising them skyward. He chanted or spoke words Peter couldn't understand. Then, to his utter disbelief, the three grabbed hands and leaped into the ravine. Peter's eyes widened in shock, unable to process what he had just seen. He was about to get out and check on the three when he felt a strange vibration beneath him.

Peter shifted in his seat, unsure if he imagined it. Before he could act, an aftershock of enormous proportions rattled the Harvester and everything around him. Peter didn't know what to do. Should he jump out and take his chances on the ground or stay in the cab? When the last one hit, debris was falling everywhere. He could certainly be hit by something that could hurt or kill him. However, if the truck went over…Mother Nature decided for him.

The road ahead gave way and collapsed into the ravine with a deafening crash. As the soil and rock crumbled, the truck's front wheels edged closer to the newly formed precipice. Peter was paralyzed by terror, clinging to the steering wheel in a death grip. Starting the truck and putting it in reverse would have been the thing to do. But his panicked brain was unable to implement that strategy.

Blanton watched helplessly as his view of the roadway disappeared. A vision of a roller coaster he once rode in San Francisco flashed through his mind. He remembered he fear as he hung at the top of the highest drop before the car plunged down the track. But this was far worse. This time, at the end of this ride, he would die.

The Harvester pitched forward and tumbled off the edge. Peter gaped out the windshield, knowing this was it. Moments earlier, he'd escaped certain death, only to be hurled back into its jaws. He began to scream an unearthly, bone-chilling wail.

The six-wheeler plummeted toward the boulder-strewn ravine floor. As it descended, the front wheels skidded along the inwardly sloped walls, keeping the truck upright. About a hundred feet from the bottom, an outcropping shaped like a ski jump jutted out thirty feet. The truck slammed into the slope, abruptly altering its trajectory from straight down to straight out.

Upon impact, Peter's body lurched upward, and his head smashed against the roof with a sickening thud. The blow snapped his mouth shut, shattering several teeth.

Blood flowed from a cut on his tongue, but he couldn't taste it—his terror overwhelmed every other sensation. Exploding truck parts flew in all directions like shrapnel from a bomb as the vehicle hurtled toward the opposite side of the crevice. Blanton, his senses dulled from the collision, could scarcely comprehend what was happening. But he knew one thing: his demise was again staring him in the face.

The boy watched as the far wall of the chasm rushed at him. The truck would smash into the granite in seconds, likely erupting in a fiery ball. But—God save him—a cave appeared in his path just before the inevitable impact. Blanton's eyes widened with hope. Maybe, just maybe, he would cheat death again.

A thin, incredulous smile formed on Peter's face as the truck soared toward the cave. But the front axle and wheels struck the cave's edge. The crash was catastrophic, ripping the cab from the chassis. The remaining compartment, a compressed and creased steel ruin, tumbled repeatedly before coming to rest well within the cavern.

Peter Blanton lay unconscious on the floor of what remained of the vehicle. He was somewhat wedged between the seat and the dashboard console. Blood flowed in a steady stream from his nose and mouth. He had cuts and scrapes on his head, legs, and arms. Blanton was an absolute mess—but, amazingly, he still lived.

CHAPTER 10

Lucky Son of a Bitch?

Before Peter regained consciousness, several vigorous aftershocks rocked the cave. Oblivious to the tremors, the truck driver remained unconscious, sprawled across the cab of his wrecked vehicle. When he finally roused, the consequences of the crash hit him like a thunderclap.

For a fleeting moment, Peter almost wished he hadn't woken up. Pain, sharp and relentless, racked his entire body. Every nerve felt as though it were ablaze. He hadn't even tried to move yet, but the sheer weight of the agony made him pray for death.

Cringing in dread, Peter attempted to lift himself from the floor. The effort sent a searing wave of pain shooting through his back and legs, forcing a sharp hiss through clenched teeth. He nearly succumbed to the urge to stay put, but he knew he needed to assess his injuries and figure out where he was.

Summoning a reserve of strength he didn't know he had, Peter managed to prop his head on the passenger seat, using his left arm as leverage. Through tear-blurred eyes, he tried to survey his surroundings. Only faint slivers of light filtered through the cave's entrance, casting just enough illumination for him to make out the wreckage around him.

"Where the hell am I?" Peter mumbled, his voice hoarse and weak.

The catastrophic experience had at first wiped his mind clean. Confused, Peter tried to piece together what happened. Then he remembered. Like being hit with a baseball bat, the memory of the crash floored him.

Wincing at the flashback, Peter closed his eyes and shook his head in disbelief. Holy shit, how am I still alive? He looked around, focusing on his surroundings, and determined he must be in the cave he'd seen before the truck collided into its entrance.

"What a damn miracle," Peter mumbled.

Peter's next goal was to free himself from the confines of the cab. Gritting his teeth, he inched his way upward. The movement was excruciating, each small adjustment triggering fresh bursts of pain. Finally, he managed to push himself onto his knees, resting his head on the passenger seat to catch his breath.

Resigned, he eventually lifted his head. "First things first," Peter whispered. With painful effort, he sat up. The movement sent new tears streaming down his face as his body protested. He stayed still, eyes clenched shut, focusing on pushing through the pain.

With slow, deliberate movements, Peter began testing his limbs. He wiggled his fingers, flexed his arms, and bent his knees, grimacing as sharp pangs coursed through him. His joints and muscles protested fiercely, but nothing appeared to be broken. Twisting his neck, he found only minor discomfort and took that as a good sign.

His mouth hurt, and his tongue throbbed. He used his finger and found jagged edges on several teeth. A couple were gone, a few chipped, and a chunk of his tongue was missing.

"Damn it," Blanton muttered, moving his tongue around. Twice, a tooth snagged, sending a sharp jolt through his brain. He sighed and shook his head. "Well, all things considered, I am one lucky son of a bitch!

Confident his body parts functioned properly, Peter decided to explore the cave. He got on the seat and pulled the passenger door handle, but it wouldn't budge. He tried several more times, but it remained stuck. Ramming his shoulder to force the door open only sent shooting pain through him, convincing him to abandon the effort.

Blanton gingerly shifted to the driver's side, grimacing with every move. He tried the door on that side, but it too was wedged shut. The cab's impact compacted the frame, sealing it tight.

Sitting back, he considered his options. Kicking out the windshield might work, though it would be difficult with his injuries. Peter stretched out to check if the glass was loose, and he could push it out and crawl through. The glass was gone. Of course, it hadn't survived the crash. After much effort, he climbed onto the console and wriggled through the empty windshield frame onto the crushed hood.

So far, so good, he thought. He scooted down to the edge, expecting to find the bumper, but the steel frame lay two hundred yards away at the bottom of the ravine. Blanton slid off the hood, lost his balance, and fell hard as his legs failed to support him. The impact sent a renewed jolt of pain through every inch of his body. His back screamed, his stomach burned, and his teeth throbbed with a vengeance.

"Motherfucker," he shouted, his voice echoing off the cave walls. He stared into the darkness and yelled again, "MOTHERFUCKER, SON OF A BITCH." The words reverberated, bouncing back at him as if a dozen voices were screaming in unison. "Oh, brother," he muttered, feeling the absurdity of his situation.

Gritting his teeth, he used the front of the cab to steady himself and rose to his feet. He took a tentative step with his right leg, but his knee buckled, nearly sending him to the ground again. Cursing, Peter leaned against the truck. After multiple attempts, he managed a halting stride with his left leg, which felt sturdier. Convinced he could stay upright, he hobbled to the cave's entrance.

Standing at the edge, he surveyed the ravine. Peter noted that shadows from the trees above already blocked much of the sun's rays. Nightfall grew near, and he needed to figure out where he was in relation to the bottom of the gorge. Leaning over the edge, Peter estimated the drop to the ravine floor to be about thirty feet. It wasn't ideal, but it seemed manageable—tomorrow. For now, he needed rest, food, and water.

Returning to the wrecked cab, a trip that took longer than it should have, Peter felt a gnawing hunger and thirst. He remembered the thermos with lemonade under his seat—his first bit of luck. He also recalled saving half a sandwich from yesterday's lunch. It wouldn't be appetizing, but it was better than nothing.

He climbed back onto the hood and began crawling toward the cab when a sound froze him in place. He whipped around, his heart racing. "Who's there?" he called out weakly. What happened next sent a new surge of fear through him.

Without warning, a small fire illuminated the cave. Standing there, lit by the flickering flames, was an Indian woman and a child, a girl. They were no more than twenty feet away, dressed in tanned deerskin, holding hands and staring at him in silence. Could this be the same Indians he'd seen before? No, not possible. Those three must be dead from the jump.

Peter was stunned. But just when he thought things couldn't get any stranger, the two Indians began screaming, their wails filled with anguish. Their clothes started to shred as if cut by invisible knives. At that moment, their heads jerked back, and wide gaping slits appeared at their throats, with blood gushing out like raging waterfalls.

Horrified, Peter threw his arms over his eyes, unable to bear the sight. He stayed that way, trembling, until the screaming stopped. When he lowered his arms, the cave was dark again, and the Indians were gone.

I must have a concussion or something, Peter thought.

He needed to get back inside the truck cab. Just as he started to move, a foul odor hit his nose, making him pause and sniff the air. The rank smell was an odor of death—maybe a dead rat or possum nearby, or perhaps he'd startled a skunk. But no, this stench reeked far worse, clinging to his nostrils like rot.

"What the fuck is that?" Peter muttered as he raised the crook of his arm to his nose and scanned the darkness. The putrid smell overwhelmed his senses, and his stomach churned, threatening to make him vomit.

Before that happened, a scraping sound echoed through the cave. It sounded like a metal pipe or chain dragging across the stone floor. A new terror replaced the urge to vomit. The metallic clatter grew louder and closer, accompanied by the foul stink that choked his breath.

Blanton's mind raced as he wondered if whatever attacked the Indians was coming for him. He turned and began to scramble back into the cab when the noise stopped. But the eerie, foreboding silence made his skin crawl. And that stench was still there.

A low, deep-throated growl broke the quiet. Peter looked toward the cave's entrance, hoping it was just thunder rolling in from outside. But the growl came again, closer this time, not from the opening but from deeper within the cave. Someone or something lurked in the darkness.

"No, no, no!" Peter stammered, trying to pull himself into the wrecked cab. He banged his head on the roof, causing a gash on his forehead. Blood streamed down his face, blinding his right eye, but he didn't stop. Summoning every ounce of strength, he attempted to claw his way in when something cold and unyielding grabbed his leg.

A razor-sharp grip tore through his pants like scissors through tissue paper and sunk into his flesh. He shrieked in pain. The thing holding him answered his cry with its own thunderous howl. The sound resounded off the stone walls, a heinous rumbling unlike anything Peter had ever heard.

Blanton's bowels let loose, and a torrent of waste poured into his pants.

Ignoring this bodily dysfunction, he tried to use his free leg to kick and pound at whatever held him. But flail away as he might, his efforts produced no relief. In fact, instead of finding his way back inside the truck, he was being dragged away from its hopeful haven.

Grabbing at anything he could, he latched onto a wrinkled gash in the hood. His fingers wrapped around the fold, the metal slicing into his hand. The burning from the cut hurt like hell, but this agony went unnoticed as panic gripped most of his bodily sensations, deadening all feelings except the urgency to get free.

Up to this point, Peter had been on his stomach. In the grasp of God knew what, he rolled onto his back with the intent to kick the shit out of his attacker's face. What he saw, the last thing he would ever see, almost stopped his heart then and there.

Above him towered a beast so hideous and petrifying that Blanton wished he'd died in the accident. Even with the limited light, he could tell the fiend stood over fifteen feet tall, with an enormous, misshapen head well out of proportion to its body.

Tentacles, reminiscent of Medusa's snakes from ancient Greek tales, sprouted from where its ears should have been. They wiggled and squirmed like flopping eels. Metallic-looking scales, each the size of a dinner plate, covered its frame. The monster's arms emerged near the neck and rolled down muscularly, ending in claw-like fists.

Peter couldn't see the creature's legs, but that didn't matter. What he could see loosened his bowels again and sent his heart into spasms. The beast's red eyes glowed like fiery embers, pulsating with each foul, putrid breath it took.

The two combatants now stared face-to-face. Blanton was paralyzed with terror while the monster appeared indifferent to the trembling man in its grasp. Peter continued trying to push and pull his way back into the truck, but the creature held him in place as if toying with a weightless rag doll.

Neither Blanton nor the giant moved for several long, agonizing moments. A tug-of-war existed with no winner. Peter quaked with fright, and though he didn't realize it, he was sobbing. Time seemed to drag on like sludge through tar.

Then, something occurred that Peter couldn't believe possible: the thing spoke. In a deep, husky growl, it said, "You are one of them. I can smell the rancid ancestry running through your veins."

Peter gulped hard and opened his mouth to speak. He had no idea what the creature meant by its words but knew this had to be a huge misunderstanding. Before he could argue with the monster, a clawed talon seized his left arm. The grip wasn't aggressive and didn't pierce his skin like when his leg had been grabbed, but it froze Peter solid.

The monster's massive head tilted. It appeared as though he was studying his captive. Peter kept his gaze on the glowing, red-eyed face. But his terror and the beast's putrid breath were almost too much for him to bear.

Just when the boy thought the stalemate might last forever, the demon turned its eyes away and focused on the arm it held. Peter watched in trepidation as the creature seemed to contemplate the appendage in its grasp. And then, without any warning, it yanked Peter's arm off. The move was effortless. His limb ripped out of its socket like someone plucking a puff of cotton candy from its cone.

A scream erupted, echoing through the cavern. It might have been heard for miles—if any other human had been around to hear it. It was one of the most horrific, primal sounds ever to pierce Peter's ears. But what horrified him more was that he was the one screaming.

The hellish monster ignored the high-pitched shriek as it shoved half of Blanton's arm into its mouth. It bit down, severing the appendage just below the elbow. For a moment, it seemed to be testing the flavor. Its jaw ground and gnawed for several seconds. Blanton's flesh and bone must have been at least palatable as the rest of the limb followed into the cavernous mouth.

Though blood pumped from Blanton's arm in roiling uncontrolled gushes, he remained semi-conscious—and screaming. The monster seemed to get annoyed by the ear-piercing sounds. It opened its mouth and chomped, severing the orb cleanly from Peter's neck and swallowing it whole.

Blanton's body jerked a few times before going limp. The beast chewed its latest tidbit, swallowed, and then turned and faded into the cave's inner workings, dragging the lifeless remains of Peter Blanton with it.

****

Taylor Benson offered a reward for information about the lost boy and his truck, but no response to the offer was ever provided. Peter Blanton had evaporated like a puff of smoke.

Though no correlation was established, several other people in other parts of California and other states mysteriously vanished that day. All had relatives who had participated in the Wiyot massacre of 1860.

CHAPTER 11

The Hunter Becomes the Hunted

February 22, 1950

The Forest Near Orca

Kenny Tucker and his Labrador, Butch, followed a blood trail through the forest, their footsteps silent on the damp earth. Kenny had aimed perfectly, hitting the eight-point buck in the right shoulder. The deer had collapsed mid-run, its tawny hide pierced by the bullet from Kenny's Remington 141 Gamemaster.

It should've been an easy finish. Go to the animal, gut it, and then haul it home— a triumphant provider for his family. But to his disbelief, the stag defied death, leaping back to its feet and vanishing into the dense woods.

"What the heck? Damn it. Get after him, Butch, don't lose him!" Kenny yelled as he sprinted after his Lab. The forest around them thickened, but Butch, an expert tracker, never slowed. He weaved through the underbrush with ease, his nose low to the ground, following the blood scent.

Kenny had raised Butch from a pup, the two forming an inseparable bond over four years of hunting together. Kenny, once a wiry teenager, had grown into a sturdy six-foot-tall young man, and Butch had grown into a powerful seventy-pound Labrador. Together, they were one of the best hunter tracker pairs in Humboldt County.

But in recent months, the deer population had inexplicably thinned. The scarcity made this buck all the more important— a prize that could feed his family for weeks. Kenny felt a surge of determination but also a creeping unease as they pushed deeper into the forest.

As he followed Butch, something gnawed at the back of his mind—an unease he couldn't shake. The deeper they went into the woods, the more the atmosphere seemed to change.

It wasn't just the dense canopy of redwoods that made the forest feel darker. It was the silence. The forest itself seemed to be holding its breath. The usual chorus of birds and rustling critters had vanished, replaced by an oppressive stillness. Only Butch's panting and the occasional crack of twigs beneath Kenny's boots broke the silence.

Something flickered in the corner of Kenny's vision—a flash of movement, a blur of color running parallel to him. He froze, raising his rifle, eyes scanning the dense foliage. The shadows seemed to stretch and shift, but he saw nothing.

"Who's there?" Kenny called, his voice wavering. His finger hovered over the trigger. Silence answered, and after a long moment, he lowered the weapon. His pulse thundered in his ears. Maybe it was just his imagination, the adrenaline making him jumpy. But the feeling of being watched lingered, growing stronger with every step.

Butch let out a wild bark ahead, snapping Kenny out of his thoughts. He resumed his pace, following the Lab deeper into the woods. But now, with every step, he felt the weight of unseen eyes watching him. Someone—or something—was shadowing him.

The trail soon gave way to a clearing where Butch stood panting eagerly. But there was no sign of the buck. Kenny knelt to inspect the ground. The trail was faint but clear—blood droplets and hoofprints leading toward a massive fallen redwood spanning a deep gorge.

Kenny swore under his breath. The deer had crossed into Orca territory.

His father had always warned him about this place, about the strange things that happened here. He'd been told stories of people who had disappeared near Orca over the years, vanishing without a trace. His father's warnings echoed in his mind: Stay away from that town and the woods around it. They're cursed, boy.

But there was venison over the bridge—enough to keep his family fed through the rest of the winter. Kenny squared his shoulders, unwilling to let his father's tales spook him into giving up.

"Come on, Butch," he muttered, climbing onto the tree. "We've come this far."

Butch hesitated, his tail tucked low, eyes fixed on his owner. He let out a soft whine, his body tense.

"What's wrong, boy? Scared of a little tree?" Kenny tried to sound confident, though the knot in his stomach betrayed him. He crouched, giving Butch an encouraging pat. "Come on. It'll hold."

Together, they made their way across, the wind whistling through the gorge below. Once they reached the other side, Kenny knelt to search for tracks. Butch walked over to his side and began to growl, staring into the trees.

"What is it, boy?" Kenny whispered, clutching his rifle. The breeze shifted, and a strange, sickly stench wafted through the air, making Kenny wince and cover his nose with the crook of his arm. He stood and scanned the darkened woods, his pulse quickening. And then, a rustling noise came from the underbrush, and Butch bolted forward.

"Butch! Come back here!" Kenny hissed, his voice barely above a whisper. He chased after the dog, but the tee canopy was so thick that it blotted out most of the sunlight, casting the forest in near darkness. Sweat trickled down his forehead as he pushed through the ferns and low-hanging branches.

A tremendous crash echoed through the trees ahead, then another. It sounded as though something enormous was charging through the woods. Kenny froze. Moments later, Butch came barreling out of the underbrush, tail tucked, his body shaking.

"What the hell…" Kenny muttered. The crashing grew louder—and closer. He raised his rifle, every muscle in his body taut with fear. And then, an Indian woman and a young girl emerged from the trees. They moved with caution, almost trance-like, their faces expressionless.

Kenny froze, staring at them in confusion. "Who are you? Are you lost?" he asked, lowering his weapon.

The woman and girl didn't respond. And then they pointed at him and began to scream, their faces contorting in pain. Kenny took a step back, his heart in his throat.

Without warning, their heads snapped backward as if yanked by invisible hands. Deep gashes opened across their throats, blood pouring down their chests. Kenny's breath hitched as he watched in horror.

A deafening roar erupted from somewhere in the forest. The ground beneath him seemed to tremble.

"Holy Jesus!" The hunter cried. He didn't wait to see what kind of beast made the noise. Forgetting the deer, forgetting the hunt, Kenny turned and bolted for the fallen tree—toward the safety of the other side—toward home—deer or no deer.

Butch was already halfway across the bridge, barking frantically as Kenny ran. The young hunter pushed himself harder, his legs burning, breath coming in ragged gasps. The tree was only twenty feet away. He was going to make it.

Then, something cold and sharp clamped around his neck.

The young hunter screamed, but the sound was cut off as he was yanked backward, his body slamming to the ground with a sickening thud. His vision swam, but through the blur, he saw it—a hulking, monstrous figure with eyes that burned like embers in the dark. Jagged teeth glistened as the beast's breath wafted over him, foul and hot.

With one powerful motion, the creature lifted Kenny off the ground. He kicked and thrashed, but it was no use. The last thing he saw was the beast's mouth descending on him before darkness consumed him.

Butch, still perched on the redwood bridge, barked desperately in protest, but to no avail, as the monster disappeared into the shadows, dragging what remained of Kenny Tucker with it.

That same day, throughout Humboldt County and beyond, people vanished. Families with names like Hurley, Johnson, Peterson, Taylor, and Blanton were struck by bizarre disappearances and violent deaths. No one would ever connect these events, but the horrors of Orca and its cursed woods had begun again.

CHAPTER 12

Consequences

December 25th, 1959

Manaus, Brazil

Wes Cravenfish's right eyelid opened a slit, then closed. "Oh my God," he groaned, raising his right hand to his face. He tried to do the same with his left hand but couldn't; something heavy pinned it down. His right eyelid opened again, and with effort, the left followed. He used his free hand to rub away the sleep—and the hangover. The sleep began to slip away, but the hangover remained fully in place.

Cravenfish realized he was in a bed—but not his bed. This wasn't his apartment; that was obvious. Slowly, he turned his head and saw why he couldn't move his arm: a person was lying on it.

The figure beside him faced away, giving no clue to their identity. He glanced around the room, his confusion growing. Brightly painted walls. Horse trophies. Elegant, expensive furniture. A dressing table with mirror. It looked to be a woman's room. But whose?

Suddenly, his bladder screamed for relief. Gently, he pulled his arm out from under the person. It was no easy task.

A soft moan. A woman's moan. That was a good sign. Cravenfish rolled over and moved a clump of the woman's hair from her face.

"Oh shit," he muttered. It was Celia, Pablo Estefan's daughter.

How the hell did he end up in her bed? He gazed down at her face, and despite his rising panic, he couldn't help but appreciate that she was one of the most beautiful women he'd ever seen. But she was his employer's daughter, and he'd been warned—repeatedly—to stay away.

Wes groaned as he leaned back down. How had this happened? As the fog from the previous night began to lift, fragmented memories surfaced.

Christmas Eve. Wes remembered that much. Christmas Eve was the big celebration in Brazil. It was the night families came together to exchange gifts and enjoy a traditional feast. Estefan had invited him to join his family for the festivities, knowing he had no relatives nearby.

"Christ. I'm in Pablo Estefan's house and in his only daughter's bed," Wes muttered, the dread settling in. If he finds me here, I'm dead. I'll be dismembered and dumped in the Amazon. How the hell had he been stupid enough to end up in the most dangerous bedroom in the entire country?

He got up, careful not to jostle the bed, and headed into the bathroom. Standing on wobbly legs, he tried to piece the night together. He remembered getting dropped off by a taxi and meeting Estefan and his wife at the door. He mingled with the family, trying to fit in despite his shaky Spanish. He mostly kept to himself, avoiding uncomfortable situations—and avoiding Celia—at all costs. So how the hell had he ended up here?

He vaguely recalled dessert and a few drinks—alone. After that, things got fuzzy.

"Boy, you've done it this time. This is not good," Wes muttered, staring at his image in the mirror. "If you don't want this to be your last day on earth, you better split now." He gathered his clothes—underwear, pants, shirt. After getting dressed, he walked to the window to get a lay of the land. It had been dark when he arrived, so he needed to know where to go.

"Good morning, Papi," Celia whispered. Wes jumped, whirling around to find Celia watching him, her hair a tousled mess but her eyes glittering with amusement. She pulled the blanket down to her waist, the sheet slipping to reveal the curve of her bare breasts. "Come back to bed," she purred, her voice dripping with suggestion. "I want you again."

"Uh, hold on a second," Wes stammered, stepping back. "Celia, I have a couple of quick questions. How did I end up in your room? And does your father know I'm here?"

Pulling the covers up to her neck in mock modesty, Celia giggled. "Does my father know you ravaged his twenty-year-old virgin daughter all night, three doors down from his? I think not."

"Celia, please. Wait, virgin?" Wes exclaimed; eyes wide.

Celia laughed and rolled her eyes.

"Very funny. Now tell me what the hell happened."

"You're so uptight, Papi," she teased, sitting up slowly.

Wes glowered at her.

"Fine. At midnight, we exchanged gifts. It took a couple of hours—muy buena. I got some lovely things. Do you want me to show you?" She started to rise, a wicked smile on her lips.

"Celia! Stop it."

"Okay, okay." She giggled again. "You were trying to leave around two a.m., but no taxis that late. My father convinced you to stay. We have many extra rooms on the third floor. I found you on the porch with a bottle of Pappa's tequila. I think you were a little sad, sí? Anyway, you and I finished drinking it all.

"We—?" Wes motioned between the two of them, horrified. "The two of us? Alone?"

"Yes, you and me, silly. When the bottle was empty, we decided to call it a night; we were both feeling pretty good by then, I think. Somehow, we made our way to the stairs leading to the upper rooms. You walked me to my room and I, uh, well, I kissed you goodnight–just a little peck. And then I kissed you a lot. And you kissed me back. You know, you use your tongue—muy buena. And your hands, they are like a magician's. Disappearing under my dress and doing magic tricks,"

"Oh my god," Wes sighed.

Another giggle before she went on. "Si. Next thing I know, I'm in bed with you, and you make mad, passionate love to me—and I liked it. You do it over and over. You are very virile," she said, her eyes lifting in amazement. "And I like it so much I need you to return to me now. I am aching for you to— you know."

She started to pull the sheet down when a knock at Celia's door nearly stopped Wes' heart. His breath caught in his throat as Celia pressed a finger to her lips.

"Hola," she called out, her voice thick with sleep.

"Hola, Celia. Estas despierta?" Pablo's Estefan said through the door.

Wes's stomach lurched. Celia shot him a mischievous glance. "He's asking if I'm awake," she whispered, her lips curving into a grin. "So… are you coming back to bed, or should I tell Papa you're here with your big American—" Her eyes flicked to his crotch with a devilish sparkle.

"Stop! That's not funny," Wes hissed, panic rising. "Do you want to get me killed?"

"Your choice, señor," she murmured. The sheet and bedspread moved, and he could tell she was opening her legs. She seductively licked her lips and smiled.

Wes closed his eyes, grimacing. Defeated, he nodded.

"Si Pappa. Estoy despierto."

"Ah, ok. Vienes a desayunar?"

"Si, Pappa. En treinta minutos."

"Adios," Pablo said.

"Adios, Pappa," Celia said.

The two listened as Pablo's footsteps echoed down the hall.

"You've got twenty minutes before I have to get ready for breakfast," Celia grinned, pulling the covers off completely. Wes sighed, closing his eyes in resignation.

Forty minutes later, a disheveled Cravenfish slipped down the backstairs of the Estefan estate. Pausing at the bottom, he peeked through the door's glass windowpanes. Seeing no one, he bolted outside. He wanted to get as far from the house as possible. No way was he facing Pablo after this. He'd pack up and flee the country. It would be the safest thing he could do.

It was a five-mile walk back to his apartment, and with a throbbing hangover, it would feel like a death march. Wes skirted along a row of hedges, heading toward the estate's main gate. Maybe someone not named Estefan would give him a ride.

As he exited through a walkway, Wes exhaled in relief. He hadn't been seen. Thank God. If Pablo ever found out he'd slept with his daughter, Wes knew he'd lose more than just his fellowship at the National Institute of Amazonian Research. Men like Estefan had ways of making people disappear— forever and without a trace.

But just as Wes turned onto the road, an open-seated 1959 Jaguar XK was pulling into the estate.

The driver's eyes locked with his. It was Celia's mother, Maria, with Celia's grandmother in the passenger seat. Wes felt like a man caught sneaking out of a brothel. His shirt was half tucked, hair tousled, and his fly was down. All he needed was a neon sign flashing, "I just slept with your daughter."

As the car drifted by, Wes managed an awkward wave. Maria and her mother stared—expressionless. No wave. No smile. Just cold, knowing eyes. Wes's stomach churned. It was over—his time in Brazil, his career, maybe his life—all over.

****

Three days later, the disgraced scientist walked into his office at Berkeley. He was greeted as expected—termination paperwork sitting neatly on his desk. Wes regretted the outcome deeply. He loved his job, his staff, and the students he'd taught. Hell, his work in the Amazon was a once in a lifetime gig.

"Your dick finally did you in, huh, Wes?" Bob Reardon leaned against the doorway with a smirk. "Can I have your desk when they kick you out?"

Wes shot him a look, half-serious. "Take the desk. In fact, take the whole office for all I care. Not like I'll need it. But seriously, how'd you find out already?"

"Oh, the news of your dismissal was all over the campus before you'd even left Brazil. One of your "friends" on the board gleefully let that cat out of the bag," Bob said sarcastically. "All kidding aside, I'm going to miss your dumb ass. What are you going to do now?"

"Not sure. I hear a gig is available in Washington. Might go check that out."

"D.C.? The Smithsonian again?"

"Fat chance, not with what I just got canned for. No, Washington state. It's a small school near Seattle. They're looking for an archeology professor. Could be a good fit."

"Right. From prestigious Berkley University to some Podunk college no one's ever heard of. Sounds like a stellar opportunity."

"Yeah, well, I haven't decided yet," Wes scoffed as he signed the last page of his termination paperwork.

"Hey, did you hear about that discovery in Northern California?" Reardon asked, his tone casual but with a glint of excitement in his eyes.

Wes glanced up. "No. What's the story?"

"It's about a missing settlement. Hold on. Let me grab it," Bob said as he walked out of Wes' office. A few minutes later, he returned with a file. "When I got the call about it, I did some research. It concerns an area in the north, a place called Orca. A group settled there in the late '30s, but by February 1940, the entire population had vanished. An earthquake or something was the likely cause. The place is now known as the Lost Coast.

"I also found some notes on other missing people in that area over the years. I didn't have time to really dive into it, but it's all in the files," Bob said as he handed the information to Wes.

"You don't say?" Wes raised an eyebrow.

"You say that like you know something," Bob replied.

"No. At least, I don't think so." Wes said, his voice distant. "Well, anyway, Susan Blake is leading the project," Reardon said, then realized his blunder. "Sorry, man."

"It's fine. I'm way over her," Wes said, though Reardon knew better.

"Well, I'm glad to hear you're finally past it," Bob said with a touch of sarcasm.

"I doubt Susan would want me involved. She'd probably prefer I stay far away," Wes theorized, sealing the envelope with his paperwork. "Here, can you drop this off at the dean's office? I'd rather not run into him again—our last chat didn't go so well."

"No worries. Hey, if you ever get back this way, don't bother looking me up," Reardon teased and then busted out in laughter.

"You're hilarious—asshole. Okay, I'm out. I'll see you around." Wes stood, gave Reardon a quick hug, and headed out. Bob noticed Wes kept the information on Orca and smirked. "Yeah, you're way over her," he muttered, a wry smile on his face.

CHAPTER 13

Tank and Peggy

Wes left the archaeology building and walked toward his car. Halfway there, he stopped to look at the school. He'd been teaching here for more than eight years. Wes liked the job and most of the people. He was going to miss his students, and that gnawed at him. "Son of a bitch. I am such an asshole," he swore.

He reached his 1959 Porsche 356 and was about to open the door when someone called his name.

"Wesley."

"Oh God," Wes muttered under his breath. Only one person used that name besides his mother—and it wasn't out of affection. He turned to see a tall, imposing figure approaching him, her black skirt, blouse, and high-heeled shoes accentuating her statuesque frame.

"Susan. What a... surprise," Wes said, his voice trailing off.

She sighed, a half-smile playing on her lips. "Hello, Wesley. Good to see you, too. Long time, no... nothing."

"Ouch."

"Sorry. That wasn't very nice of me, was it? On second thought—it's exactly what you deserve."

"Did you come to Berkley just to chastise me or was there something else?"

They stood silent for several seconds, staring at one another until Susan spoke again. "No, I'm not here to chastise you for your deplorable past behavior. I'm looking for Bob Reardon. Is he around? There's this site…"

"Yeah, he told me. There's a new dig in Northern California," Wes interrupted. He took a moment to look her over. She was just as striking as ever. Those dark brown eyes still drew him in. Her figure? Curves in all the right places. And damn, those lips—they could've had a "welcome home" sign hanging over them.

Susan brushed a stray lock of hair from her face, revealing a small bruise on her forehead.

"Whoa. What happened to your head?" Wes asked with genuine concern.

"What," she answered, confused. "Oh, the bruise. Stupid accident, but... weird," Susan replied, touching her forehead absentmindedly.

"Weird? How so?"

"On one of our trips to the site in California, I was pulling some gear off a shelf when this terrifying roar came out of nowhere. It shook me so much that I dropped a box on my head."

"Looks like it hit you pretty good."

"I'll survive," Susan responded cooly.

Wes ignored the tone. "Must be plenty of big cats in that area. Could it have been a mountain lion?"

"That's what I thought at first, too. But…"

"But what?"

"Well, it didn't sound like any mountain lion I've ever heard. In fact, it didn't sound like any animal I've ever heard," Susan said, her voice tinged with unease. "Remember that African lion that kept taunting us from the hill above our camp in the Sahara? And how it's roar echoed through that valley?"

"Yeah, we thought it was two lions, maybe three. Turned out it was just one with some serious vocal amplification due to the natural hills around us."

"Exactly. But this roar? It was louder. More… primal. Scared the hell out of me," Susan admitted.

"And you never saw what caused it?"

"Nope. And I haven't heard it since. Weird, right? Anyway, where's Bob?"

"Oh, he's packing up. Heading to Asia for a new discovery. Leaves tomorrow night."

"What? He didn't tell me. How long will he be gone?"

"Six to nine months. Was supposed to be my gig, but then…well," Wes hesitated.

"But then what?" Susan questioned. She stared at him for several seconds and then recognized a difference in Wes' expression. "Don't tell me. You got canned, didn't you? Why? Hold it. I don't want to hear it," she said as she held up her hands.

"A simple misunderstanding. But maybe it was time to go. I've never stayed at a job this long."

"You never change, do you? Whatever. So, what's next? Do you have something lined up?"

"Oh yeah. Plenty. Got my pick of a bunch of positions," Cravenfish boasted.

"So... nothing," Susan laughed, locking eyes with him in a way that reminded him of past battles—ones he rarely won.

"Not nothing," Wes shot back, though, after a pause, he half-smiled. "Okay, close to nothing. So, what's the deal with the dig?"

"Uh... well," Susan wavered.

"Come on, we could work together again—like old times," Wes teased.

"I don't think that's a good idea. Rudy's funding the project."

"Oh, shit. Rudy Stephenson? That scumbag?"

"Funny, he called you the same thing. You two have so much in common—except he doesn't cheat on his girlfriend."
"Ugh," Wes groaned. "Who else is involved?"

"Tank Howard, Peggy Tifton, Bobby, of course, and Julia Frazier," Susan replied.

"Julia, Peggy, and Bobby? I haven't seen them in years. And Tank, too? Sounds like a bigger deal than you're letting on."

"It involves the Wiyot Indians. Oddly, everyone but me seems to have some ancestral connection to the area. Peggy and Bobby's grandfather lived nearby in the late 1800s, and he died under mysterious circumstances. Julia's great-uncle, Peter Frazier, was mayor of Ferndale in the 1930s. And Tank found out his birth parents were from Eureka."

Wes's expression changed, catching Susan's attention. "What's wrong? You look like you just swallowed a bug."

"Huh? Oh, I'm sure it's nothing," Wes mumbled.

"Spill it," Susan demanded.

"If you remember, my family is from around there too. Humboldt County, I think. It's strange, don't you think? All of us have roots there."

"All except me," Susan said, mulling over the coincidence. "Listen, I've got to go. It was...wonderful seeing you again. Good luck with...well, with whatever's next. I mean that," Susan finished, her voice tinged with emotion.

"Yeah, thanks. And good luck on the dig," Wes replied, watching her walk away. A pang of regret twisted in his chest.

At one point, Wes had thought he and Susan might go the distance. But, like all his other relationships, he'd managed to screw it up—this time, in spectacular fashion. And all because of Jennifer Sanchez.

Jennifer wasn't beautiful, but something about her was sexy. No doubt. But she also had a quiet confidence and a flirtatious charm that was hard to ignore.

Wes had never planned or wanted to cross any lines with her. In fact, he hadn't even been attracted to her as her personality often rubbed him the wrong way. But then that night happened—and it had all changed.

He had brought some data to Susan's apartment on an archaeological dig she was interested in. She was out of town, but he had offered to drop it off so she could review it when she returned. When he arrived, Jennifer was about to sit down for homemade lasagna and a Merlot.

Initially, he declined her invitation to stay and eat, but she insisted. He finally gave in. After all, he loved lasagna, and who could resist a decent California Merlot? All was going well until she asked a question that unlocked a door Wes should've slammed shut.

"Wes, are you going to marry Susan, or are you just screwing around with her?"

That was it. The floodgates opened.

Though Wes loved Susan, marriage hadn't been on his mind.

"Well, Jennifer, I, uh... Hmm. To be honest, we haven't discussed it. And, frankly, that's between her and me."

With Frank Sinatra's Come Fly with Me playing in the background, Jennifer wouldn't let it go. She grilled Wes through two and a half bottles of wine. That's when the somewhat attractive Jennifer Sanchez became slightly more appealing. When she excused herself to change into "something more comfortable," Wes's compass lost its true north.

She returned wearing a West Point football jersey that just reached her thighs. Even when dressed, Jennifer's well-toned legs and curvaceous figure were alluring. Now, with almost nothing on, Wes found his self-control waning.

Jennifer grabbed her wine, glanced at Wes, and then sat down on the couch, her jersey riding up just enough to eliminate any pretense of modesty.

"Come sit with me," she said, patting the cushion. "Let's finish this last glass."

Wes could've said no. He should have. But the rising erection in his pants took over all reason. He walked around the coffee table and sat down. And that's when Jennifer pounced.

She pushed him back on the couch, climbed on top of him, and hovered over his crotch. It was immediately confirmed by a glaring visual—Jennifer wasn't wearing anything under the sweatshirt. Her clean-shaven pubic area, a trend sparked by the rise of bikinis in the '40s, finished off what little resolve Wes had left.

When Cravenfish sobered up, the devastation of what happened hit him. He knew he'd been seduced, but he could've said no. He should've said no. The guilt drained him of all his moral pride. But that wasn't the worst part.

Jennifer had done it for a reason.

When Susan returned from her trip, Jennifer was waiting. Her roommate confessed everything by claiming she did her a favor by exposing Wes as a cheat. Two things happened: Susan punched Jennifer in the nose, severing their friendship, and then called Wes. She screamed every explicit detail Jennifer had described before hanging up and ending their relationship. Wes tried to apologize, many times, but no excuse or apology could repair the damage.

****

When Wes arrived home from Berkeley, he tossed his briefcase on the couch and set his box of office items on the dining room table. He grabbed a beer from his Frigidaire and pulled out the file on the California discovery. The packet included notes gathered from interviews with local Wiyot tribe members, accounts from settlers, and research documents from the Humboldt County Courthouse archives. All of it had been summarized in a brief.

Wes read:

Around the turn of the 19th century, whispers spread about a remote but awe-inspiring region in Northern California. Tales of lush landscapes brimming with wildlife and natural resources reached the ears of explorers and settlers alike. Towering centuries-old Redwoods were said to stand as sentinels over this hidden land.

Perched atop cliffs that rose hundreds of feet above the Pacific Ocean, the plateau offered breathtaking vistas. Yet, despite the rumors, no one seemed to know its exact location, and over time, the area became more myth than reality—a fairytale whispered among wanderers.

It wasn't until retired World War I veteran Colonel Trevor Donaldson visited Humboldt County and heard these tales firsthand that someone believed in the stories. The description of this untouched paradise sounded like the place Donaldson had been searching for, and soon, he launched an expedition to locate the land.

Donaldson spent weeks chasing dead ends. Dozens of inquiries led nowhere—and then he met a Wiyot chieftain willing to talk. The craggy-faced leader related tales of an unparalleled landscape: vast grasslands, freshwater springs, and abundant wildlife. It was everything Donaldson had envisioned, but the chief also issued a grave reproach: an evil spirit guarded the bluff, a devilish beast that devoured all who trespassed. He urged Donaldson not to go, claiming anyone who ventured there would never return.

At first, the Colonel dismissed the warning as tribal superstition. Yet, during one conversation, the chief suddenly grabbed his arm with surprising force. His eyes were wide, ablaze with unmitigated fear. He repeated his caution, insisting that death awaited any who dared to enter the sacred land.

Donaldson remained undeterred. To him, the area held too much promise. He confided in his plans with George McNally, the mayor of Capetown. Donaldson envisioned a self-sufficient colony that could stand isolated from the world should another global conflict break out again. Many war veterans who had served under Donaldson shared this vision and joined him in his quest.

Using a hand-drawn map the reluctant Wiyot chief had provided, Donaldson and his men navigated rough-hewn roads and animal trails. The journey was arduous, but the map indicated they were close. Then they hit an obstacle: a foot deep ravine, a natural moat encircling the land.

They searched for a way across the chasm for hours, almost ready to give up. Then, by sheer luck, they stumbled upon a narrow clearing where the gap between the cliffs was manageable. With renewed energy, they built a temporary footbridge, eager to explore the area beyond the ravine.

Once on the other side, it didn't take long for Donaldson's group to realize the legends were true. Towering oak, pine, and redwood trees thrived throughout the landscape, offering more than enough timber for building homes. Signs of wildlife— deer, wild boar, game fowl—were abundant. Though rugged, the land appeared fertile for farming, and freshwater springs trickled from nearby hills. It was everything they had hoped for.

After hours of trekking through dense scrub and pine, they came across something unexpected: a broad, well-trodden animal trail. It was too large to be made by deer or bear. The men exchanged puzzled glances but were grateful for the easier passage. They followed the path for a few hundred yards until the trees gave way to a stunning sight: a vast meadow stretched out at least fifty acres wide before them. The land was primarily flat, with gentle hills rolling toward the horizon, covered in tall, flowing grasses.

And beyond it, the Pacific Ocean.

The men stood at the edge of a massive cliff, mesmerized by its grandeur. Below, black sand beaches shimmered in the sun to their left, reflecting like diamonds. To their right, waves crashed against colossal boulders, sending plumes of spray high into the air. It was a paradise.

One odd discovery, however, marred their sense of ownership: an old, weather-beaten hut. Inside were beds of bear hide and deer-skin clothing for a man, woman, and child. It was strange, almost eerie, but they considered it an abandoned home and ignored the site.

Donaldson claimed the land and christened it Orca after the majestic whales that migrated along the coast.

Over the next six months, the settlement took shape. Donaldson's community of war veterans and their families threw themselves into building a new life. Log homes were erected, a general store opened, and even a tiny church stood in the center of town. A blacksmith's shop hammered out tools, and the settlers built corrals for livestock, sties for pigs, and coops for chickens. By the spring of 1939, Orca was thriving.

The settlers were overjoyed with their new home, perched high above the roaring Pacific. One colonist declared, "We are as close to God as possible and far from outsider influence. It is heaven on earth."

By the fall of that year, Europe was again in turmoil, and whispers of another war reached American shores. Yet, for the settlers of Orca, it was as if they were in their own world—isolated, protected.

Then, in February of 1940, Orca fell silent.

Months passed, and there was no word from the settlement. People who had known about the colony began to worry—had something gone wrong? A small group of concerned citizens went to the ravine, but they found the bridge that crossed the span destroyed.

Humboldt County officials built a temporary bridge, but when they reached Orca, no one was there. The town still stood, but all inhabitants were missing.

In the end, the community of Orca vanished as it had appeared—in mystery. No survivors ever emerged. The town was eventually forgotten, a ghost story lost to time—its only legacy whispered among the few who still remembered.

****

Cravenfish spent over an hour reading other details of the area spanning almost one hundred years. Besides Donaldson's group, he found multiple accounts of unexplained disappearances of people who traveled to or near Orca. The stories of those missing were odd, to say the least.

Wes tossed the report aside, shaking his head in disbelief. How did all these people vanish without a trace? A massive earthquake could have done in the people of Orca, but not all the others. He stood up and moved into the kitchen, craving a distraction and a snack. As he peered into his nearly empty fridge, the phone rang, cutting through the silence of his apartment.

He turned his head and stared at the ringing receiver, considering whether to answer or ignore it. After hesitating, he closed the fridge door and picked up the receiver.

"Yeah," Wes grunted into the phone, his voice still gruff from too much coffee and too little sleep.

"Wes, it's Susan," came the person on the other end, sharp with urgency.

Cravenfish's eyebrows shot up in surprise. "Wow. Miss me already?" he joked, his automatic defense mechanism kicking in.

There was a brief silence on the line, and when Susan spoke again, her voice cracked. "Tank and Peggy… They're missing.

The lightness in his tone evaporated. "What? What do you mean they're missing?"

"They were scouting a location near Orca looking for more clues about the inhabitant's disappearance. They never came back. The others searched for them for hours, but all they found were some of Tank's tools and Peggy's backpack… and… and…" Susan's speech trembled, and for a moment, she was too choked up to continue. Finally, she got out, "There was blood, Wes. A lot of blood. On the trees, on the bushes."

Wes felt a cold chill creep up his spine. "What? Okay, how long have they been missing?"

"They left early this morning," Susan continued, her words coming faster now. "It's after dark now, and they were supposed to be back by sundown at the latest. Even if they planned to stay overnight, they would've taken provisions. They didn't have anything like that with them, Wes. Nothing."

"Jesus," Wes muttered, running his hand over his face. He leaned against the kitchen counter, trying to wrap his mind around the situation. "Did you contact the authorities? Maybe the sheriff or something?"

Susan let out a bitter laugh. "I tried. Capetown is the nearest town. The police chief is a complete ass. I called him, and he said the area was 'out of his jurisdiction.' Some kind of no-man's land because of its remoteness. Total bullshit. To be honest, I think he's just scared.

"Before we went to the site, we did some research. Checked town records, talked to locals, all the things we normally do. A few of the older residents confided that a wild animal of some sorts roams the plateau. Said no one will go, including the police."

Wes squeezed his eyes shut, trying to process everything. Missing friends. Blood on the trees. A police chief too afraid to do anything. And rumors about a beast? This was insane.

"Shit," he muttered under his breath. "Okay. What do you need from me?"

There was a long pause before Susan answered. Her voice softened, almost pleading. "I'm leaving at dawn. I want you to come with me. I want someone I trust, and... Wes, I'm asking for your help. Please."

Wes hesitated. His past relationship with Susan flashed in his mind—a complicated, messy tangle of unresolved emotions, hurt, and grudges. He wasn't certain if helping her now was the best idea, but the sound of her voice—genuine fear and concern—pulled at something inside him.

Finally, he exhaled in resolve. "I'm not sure what I can do... but yeah, okay. I'll come. Just tell me where to meet you."

"I'll pick you up at 7 a.m. Give me your address. And Wes... thank you."

After hanging up the phone, Wes stood in the middle of his dimly lit kitchen, staring blankly at the receiver in his hand. Tank and Peggy weren't just coworkers. They were his friends, people he shared meals with, laughed with and lived with on expeditions. The idea of them being in danger—or worse—gnawed at his insides.

He glanced over at the stack of papers on the table—the same report he'd been reading moments earlier about Orca. What had been a historical mystery, a ghost story, now felt far too real. And personal.

CHAPTER 14

Day of Reckoning

"Is that all you're bringing? We could be gone for a week or more," Susan said, arching an eyebrow as she opened the trunk for Wes to stow his gear.

"A week or more?" Wes repeated, his frown deepening as he glanced at his small duffel bag. "I thought you were talking about a couple of days." He tugged at the bottom of his T-shirt, self-conscious about his light packing. "I've got enough. Let's go."

Susan rolled her eyes and slammed the trunk shut. "And your rifle? You've packed almost no clothes, but you're bringing a gun?"

"I heard the words 'vicious wild animal.' I'm bringing my rifle and my pistol," Wes said as he loaded both weapons into the car, his tone matter-of-fact.

Susan sighed, deciding not to argue. They got into her Saab and headed out, the silence between them settling in like an unwelcome passenger. As they merged onto US 101, the engine's hum and the tires' rhythmic thud became the only sounds filling the car. Tension hung in the air, thick with unsaid words and unresolved pain.

For the next hour, they drove north, the coastal landscape flickering by in a blur of green and gray. Neither of the car's passengers said a word Finally, Susan broke the silence, her tone sharper than intended. "Why?"

Wes glanced at her, confused. "Excuse me?"

"Why did you have to screw Jennifer?" she said, her voice cracking slightly but firm.

"Oh, that why," Wes muttered in a strangled whisper. He fell silent momentarily, gazing out the window as the scenery blurred past. Then, breaking the silence, he added, "I know this might not matter to you now, but it was the biggest mistake I've ever made."

Susan's eyes remained fixed on the road; her knuckles white as she gripped the steering wheel.

"I'm not making excuses for what I did. I don't blame the alcohol, Jennifer, or anyone else. It was all on me. I let... well, I let the wrong part of me make decisions that night." He exhaled, running his hand through his hair. "I hurt you, and I've regretted it every damn day since. I'm sorry, Susan. I've said it before, but I'll say it again. I'm so sorry."

Susan kept her gaze ahead, silent except for the tear slipping from the corner of her eye and rolling down her cheek. She wiped it away quickly, but the pain remained evident in the tightness of her jaw. Susan drove for several more minutes, the weight of Wes's apology hanging like a guillotine ready to fall.

When she next spoke, her voice was soft but steady. "Wes, I know you're sorry. I've always known that. But... it doesn't change anything. You broke my heart, and I'm not sure how to forgive you. I loved you. And you threw it away—for her." She spat the word out like it left a bad taste in her mouth. "She wasn't even—"

"I know," Wes interrupted, his response almost a murmur. "It was a stupid, selfish, reckless decision."

"Reckless doesn't begin to cover it," Susan said bitterly. "You ruined us, Wes. And I still can't understand why."

"I wish I could explain it, but I can't. I was an idiot. A total idiot."

Susan's voice shook with a mixture of anger and hurt. "There are days when I still want to pull over, grab something heavy, and bash your head in for it."

"Ouch," Wes muttered, flinching. He opened his mouth to offer something—anything—to make it better, but nothing came. Instead, he turned his head and stared out the window again, feeling the sting of her words echo in his chest.

For over an hour, they didn't speak. Wes stole glances at Susan from time to time, her profile etched in concentration and pain. Each time, a surge of regret coursed through him, and the realization hit him like a gut punch. You destroyed it all.

The landscape outside grew more rugged as they drove deeper into the wilderness. Towering pines loomed on either side of the road, casting long shadows that danced across the car's hood. Wes's thoughts drifted from their wrecked relationship to the task ahead—Orca. Tank and Peggy were missing. Blood on the trees. The unsettling feeling gnawed at his insides.

He finally broke the silence. "Do you think they're okay?"

Susan continued to stare forward, her reply barely above a whisper. "I don't know. I hope so. But something about this place... it feels wrong."

Wes nodded, a chill running down his spine. He now believed there was far more happening in Orca than either of them knew. It felt like the past and present were converging, and the weight of that realization settled heavily on both.

CHAPTER 15

Echoes of Vengeance

US 101

Northern California

Ten miles outside of Capetown

"What an asshole," Wes mumbled sleepily.

"Excuse me?" Susan shot back, her head snapping in his direction.

"Huh?" Wes blinked, still groggy, as he tried to shake off the remnants of sleep. "Oh… sorry, I think I was dreaming. What did I say?"

"You called me an asshole," Susan replied, her tone laced with annoyance.

"No, not you," Wes mumbled, rubbing his face with both hands. "I was dreaming about someone else, though I can't remember who. Where are we?"

Susan shot him a skeptical look but decided to let it slide. "We're about twenty minutes from Capetown. I'm stopping for gas and some snacks. There's a station coming up."

A few minutes later, she pulled into a Gulf station and parked by the pumps. Wes stepped out, yawning, and began filling the tank. Meanwhile, Susan went inside and picked up two Frosty Root Beers, a couple of bags of chips, sandwiches, and some candy bars.

Wes watched her through the window as the fuel gauge frantically spun on the pump, his mind drifting back to the last time they'd been together. The memory played out like a scene from a movie: Susan, in a fit of rage, tossing his belongings out of her two-story apartment window—shirts, shoes, pants, socks—all fluttering down in a cascade of angry words he was sure her mother would faint if she heard.

Suddenly, a subdued voice snapped him out of his thoughts. Wes turned to see an old man standing beside him. The man wore traditional Native American attire—a war bonnet of feathers, beads, and shells, and deerskin garb. He had tattoos covering his forehead. The sight was unexpected, jarring even.

The man gestured westward, speaking in a language Wes didn't recognize. It felt like he was supposed to know what the man was saying, but Wes shook his head, confused. "I'm sorry, I don't understand. Do you speak English?"

The old man's eyes, cloudy and bloodshot, locked onto his. After a long pause, he pointed toward the distant mountains and the Pacific Ocean. "I am Ki-ne-ti-tah, Wiyot Shaman. The last of the Wiyot murderers will face Puchúri-ghúrru's wrath, and our revenge will be fulfilled," he said, his voice deep and hollow.

Wes's heart skipped a beat. "What? Revenge for what?" he asked, his confusion deepening.

"One hundred years ago, the white man massacred our people—Wiyot men, women, and children. I have known who these killers are and have slowly eliminated them. Now, Puchúri-ghúrru will devour all who remain. Their family legacies will end, as I promised. Our people's vengeance will be complete."

Wes's blood ran cold. "Wait... when you say, 'our people,' you mean your people, right? And who... who is Puchúri-ghúrru?"

"Wes? Who are you talking to?" Susan called out as she exited the gas station.

Wes turned to her with an odd smile. "This guy here— he's saying something about death, revenge, and some spirit devouring souls. He mentioned someone named Puchúri something. I don't know, maybe he's some kind of nut."

Susan frowned as she walked to the car. "Who?" She glanced around, confused. "Who's talking about revenge and death? And did you say Puchúri-ghúrru?"

"Yeah, this guy," Wes said, gesturing to where the Indian had been standing. But the old man was gone. Wes scanned the area, eyes wide. "He was just here. Right here."

Susan stared at the space, clearly skeptical. "Wes, there's no one here. Are you trying to be funny? Because joking while our friends are missing isn't funny."

"I'm not joking!" Wes snapped. "I swear, there was a guy right here—an Indian shaman. He said his name was Ki-netaty or something. He talked about that Puchu guy and his revenge for the Wiyot massacre. I'm not making this up."

Susan gave him a long, incredulous look. "Wes, there's no one here."

Cravenfish ran his hand through his hair, frustrated. He took off and jogged toward the edge of the gas station. But there was nothing—no footprints, no trace of anyone. He circled the building, checking around the back, and returned a few minutes later, breathless.

Susan sat in the car, watching him through the windshield with a raised eyebrow. When he slid into the passenger seat, she crossed her arms, her expression demanding an explanation.

"Spill it. What's going on?" she demanded.

"Susan, I swear, that may have been the strangest thing I've ever experienced," Wes said, his voice strained. "There was an Indian standing right there, in full traditional attire. He told me he was a Wiyot shaman. He started speaking in what I assume was his native tongue, then switched to perfect English. He talked about revenge and that this Puchuri spirit had been devouring the descendants of the white men who killed his people."

"You mean Puchúri-ghúrru? And the 1860 Indian Island Massacre of the Wiyot tribe?" Susan asked, her expression serious.

"Yes, I guess so," Wes answered, shrugging his shoulders slightly.

To this point, Cravenfish had been staring out the front windshield. Now, he turned to face his past lover. With a sincerity Susan once found endearing, he said, "This is beyond strange. Kind of scary, in fact. I'm telling you; the man was as real as you and me, yet he seems to have vanished into thin air. Susan, something weird is going on."

Susan stared at him, her skepticism wavering. "I'm not saying I believe you, and I'm not saying I don't. But come on, Wes—a Wiyot shaman in full dress, here one minute and gone the next? And you do know most Wiyot shamans were women, right? So even that doesn't make sense."

"Not in a minute. He disappeared in the blink of an eye. And no, I didn't know about the women shamans. Regardless, there's no way he could've left so fast. What the hell is going on?" Wes shook his head, clearly rattled. "Maybe I'm losing my mind. Forget it. We should focus on finding Tank and Peggy."

"Let's hope finding them is easier than figuring out whatever just happened," Susan said. As they pulled back onto the road, she added, "But something you said has me thinking. The Wiyot believed in an apparition called Puchúri-ghúrru. Legend says the shamans could summon him to punish their enemies. He would appear out of nowhere and devour their bodies and souls. How did you know about him?"

"Me? I didn't know anything about him. Never heard of him until the Indian said his name."

"Think, Wes. In all your studies, are you sure you've never heard of him?"

"I'm sure. Not a name I'd forget."

"Hold on," Susan said abruptly. "I do remember you talking about this before. A couple of years ago, you mentioned that the Cravenfish ancestors came from northern California. We were at some little bar in the middle of nowhere, and you said you researched them. Could you have read about Puchúrighúrru then?"

"I did investigate my heritage. But my research came up empty. I didn't find any relationship with the Wiyot, so I didn't dig too deep into them or their religious beliefs. I found some information dating back to the turn of the century, but it stopped there. And nothing about a body and soul-devouring spirit. That I would have remembered."

"Well, what did you discover about your family tree?" Susan pressed.

Wes frowned. "Only that they were of Indian ancestry and lived somewhere in Humboldt County. But the records for many of these people are not great. And there were a dozen tribes or more living there. The only noteworthy thing I unearthed was that some of my family members spoke a form of Algonquian. But that only narrowed it down to a few tribes. Honestly, I couldn't uncover much about my history, but what I am sure of is this—I saw this guy."

"Some researching fiend you turned out to be. Couldn't find out anything about his own heritage."

"Ha, ha. Very funny. There just wasn't much documentation to research. And I had so many other things going on I couldn't take the time to dig into it. What can you tell me about the history of the region?"

Susan grimaced and said, "Well, this won't surprise you. In the late 1800s, white settlers decided they didn't want Indians as neighbors. Though the natives were there first, the newcomers believed they "discovered" the area and staked a claim to the land.

"Then, sometime in February of 1860, the settlers gathered and decided to rid the "pests" infecting the land. They coordinated a bunch of attacks on the local tribes in and around Humboldt County. Using axes, knives, and guns, they slaughtered around 250 Indians. Men, women, and children."

"Jesus," Wes muttered, shaking his head. "So, it wasn't revenge or anything? Just cold-blooded murder?"

"You got it. The Wiyot were a peaceful tribe. They did nothing to provoke what was done to them. It was after the Gold Rush and the settlers didn't want to share the wealth," Susan said.

"So, that was in February of 1860?"

"Yeah."

"Huh. A bit strange," Wes said as he scratched at his chin.

"Why strange?" Susan asked, glancing at him.

"Hold on," Wes said as he reached over his seat and retrieved his briefcase. "I remember reading about some incidents in the area, and that date seems familiar." Rifling through the case, he pulled out some books and papers. He scanned them briefly and said, "Ok, this is getting stranger by the minute."

"What do you mean?"

"Well, there are some gaps, but check this out. In late February of 1880, several leaders of the 1860 massacre vanished after a trip to scout new areas for settlements. Four of the five never came back. The only survivor, Arnold Johnson, returned home early for an emergency. No one ever saw the others again."

Susan raised an eyebrow. "What else does it say?"

"The men's names were Hurley, the leader of the massacre, Tyson, Tucker, two brothers named Blanton, and the Johnson guy. When the other four didn't return, Johnson and Hurley's son, Jacob, went searching for them. They found their camp, but there was no sign of the men.

Johnson told Jacob that before he left, he and the others decided to cut some trees down to make a bridge to cross the span surrounding Orca. When they searched the crossing, those two trees were at the bottom of the ravine.

"Johnson later confessed the real reason the five men went was to kill Mary Hurley's murderer. She had been taken ten years earlier, almost to the day. They blamed a local Indian, and witnesses said they spotted a man dressed as an Indian nearby. The girl's father gathered a search party to look for Mary, but she was never found. One of the searchers died, too; his name was Ezra Taylor.

"It goes on and on. In 1890, ten years after the hunting party's disappearance, Timothy Hurley's son Jacob and his son, Peter, vanished. They went hunting and were never seen again."

Susan's eyes widened. "Are you serious?"

"Wait. Hold on. On February 26th, 1900, three men, led by a man named Dylan Frazier, disappeared after heading west toward the sea.

"On February 24th, 1910, Frazier's daughter, Pauline, and her husband vanished. The two were newlyweds and had never seen the ocean. They went on an overnight camping trip and never returned. Their campsite was found, but there was no hint of the couple. And several feathers were discovered at the site—the kind typically used in Native American headdresses."

"You're right. This is more than strange—it can't be a coincidence. People with the same last names disappear every decade, along with these... Indian sightings? Something connects all of this."

"Yeah, and it keeps on going. After a bunch of cattle got lost in the woods, Barry Tyson, the guy who owned them, and his son Aaron went looking for them. Neither they nor the cows were ever seen again. That was February 26th, 1920.

"Then, in 1940, the entire resident of Orca went missing. A massive earthquake hit, and afterward, no one could reach the town. It says local lawmen and townsfolk tried to get to them, but the only bridge leading in had collapsed into the jagged, yawning gorge below."

"Yeah, there's a deep ravine surrounding the area where the town used to be," Susan clarified.

"Get this. At the same time Orca vanished, a deliveryman named Peter Blanton disappeared. He made his stop in Capetown, but he never made it to his stop after Orca.

"Next to vanish was a boy—Kenny Tucker, who went hunting on February 24th, 1950, and never returned. And now, your team—this year, 1960." Wes leaned back, his eyes distant as he pieced it all together.

"Ok. So, we have people with the same last name, and all the disappearances happened at the beginning of a decade," Susan stated.

"Yes, but it's more than that. All these events occurred in February. And not any time in February—always during the last week of the month."

"Unbelievable," Susan muttered, shaking her head. She paused, chewing her lip before adding, "I'm not one to buy into superstition, Wes. I'm a scientist. But this... this is unsettling. Are there any other records of disappearances outside of February?"

"Not in what I've read so far. But now that I think about it—it's been exactly 100 years since the massacre. Today is February 26th—the same date as the original Wiyot massacre," Wes said, turning to Susan.

"I don't know how this is possible," Susan murmured, her voice strained. "People with last names that match those involved in the massacre. And all the disappearances happening on the anniversary of the Wiyot massacre? Someone, or something, is behind it. Maybe it's long overdue revenge for what was done to the Wiyot."

Wes stared out the window, his mind spinning. "But who... or what... could hold a grudge for a hundred years?"

Susan didn't answer. The road stretched ahead, winding through the dense forest, leading them deeper into the unknown.

CHAPTER 16

Bloodlines

36 hours earlier
Abandoned Area around Orca

"Peg?" Tank said as he walked along a tree-shaded trail, the dappled sunlight casting fleeting patterns on the ground.

"Yeah," Peggy replied, her mind drifting as she soaked in the quiet serenity around them. The cool morning air felt refreshing, the peacefulness of the plateau calming her nerves.

"Where were you before Susan asked you to help on this site?" Tank asked, glancing at her curiously.

"Mesa Verde," Peggy answered, snapping out of her reverie. "I was working with Hank Profit on a Pueblo dig. Fascinating people, those Pueblos. Ingenious engineers, too."

"Ah. Your old flame, Hank. I should have guessed," Tank chuckled.

"What the hell are you talking about? What old flame?" Peggy shot back, eyes narrowing.

"Oh, come on, Peggy. You've had a thing for him since he gave that lecture at Arizona U. Don't act like you didn't." "You're such an ass," Peggy snapped, rolling her eyes. "The guy's ten years older than me, for God's sake. And no, I never had a thing for him. Jerk."

Tank laughed. "He's over six feet tall, barely balding, still has all his teeth, and let's not forget those sideburns. Bobby said you were really into those. So, as far as I can tell, he checks off most of your dating criteria, right?"

"You and Bobby are idiots. Hank Profit, seriously? As if," she scoffed, shaking her head.

"Yeah, yeah, whatever. So, was the dig finished? Is that why you came here?" Tank shifted the conversation, sensing her irritation.

"No, the Pueblo site's a long-term project—years, at least. I'll probably head back once we're done here. But there were two reasons I came. One, because Susan asked, I'll always show up when she does. And two, this place. I had relatives who lived in the area a hundred years ago. So, I was intrigued."

Tank raised an eyebrow. "Really? Any of them still there?"

"Nope. Oddly enough, the entire clan packed up and left Humboldt County in March 1900. I've always wondered why. I thought while I was there, I'd find some answers." Her voice carried a note of both curiosity and melancholy.

"Humboldt County? No kidding."

"Yeah."

"How many left?"

"I'm not sure of the exact number, but I think around thirty, maybe more. Adults and children. My mother mentioned it once but didn't know all the details. She just said it was... mysterious."

Tank frowned. "Mysterious, how?"

Peggy sighed. "She said the reason they left was because some family members died in strange ways or just disappeared. She couldn't tell me much more. It always intrigued me, but I never found enough information to dig deeper. Then Susan called about this site, and it all came flooding back."

"Do you know where they ended up?"

"She thought somewhere near Eureka, but it was so long ago, and she wasn't sure."

Tank stopped abruptly, turning to face her. "Eureka? You're kidding, right? That's where I'm from."

"What?" Peggy blinked, surprised. "You never told me that."

Tank's face became more serious. "Well, you know I was orphaned. It's not something I like to talk about. But yeah, I grew up in Ferndale, not far from Eureka. Weird coincidence, huh? Especially considering how your family's history sounds... well, let's say familiar."

"Familiar how?" Peggy asked, her brow furrowing.

Tank hesitated, then sighed. "My parents disappeared when I was about three. They went to a sawmill in Rolph—now Fairhaven—to get lumber for a barn. They never came back. Their truck and trailer were found, but no sign of them." Peggy's eyes widened. "That's... that's so strange."

"Tell me about it. And get this—I'm pretty sure it was late February or March of 1900. And it wasn't the first time someone in our family went missing. I unearthed others that disappeared, too."

They stood in silence for a moment, their family's eerie connections hanging in the air like a dark cloud.

"You don't think..." Peggy started, her voice cautious, "Okay, I may be way overthinking this, but do you think our families were involved with the Wiyot massacre? I mean, they lived there during that time. It seems possible, right? Maybe a survivor of the massacre was getting even."

Tank shrugged, his expression hard to read. "I've thought about it. Who knows? Have you ever investigated your family's name—Tifton—to see if there's any record of their involvement?"

Peggy shook her head. "Tifton's my married name. My family name is Tucker."

"That's right," Tank nodded. He hesitated before adding, "Have you asked Bobby? He might know something."

Peggy snorted. "Half-brother. And no, I doubt he knows more than I do."

"Well, this keeps getting better and better. I've known you for half your life and am just now discovering all this juicy stuff. I can't wait to hear what's next. So, Bobby's your half-brother. How did that come about?"

"Yep," Peggy confirmed. "My dad had an affair with a woman named Peterson. She was a widow who followed my family when they moved. Her husband died before the move, but I don't know the details. When Bobby showed up, the affair became public, and my mom almost left my dad. She didn't, though, because she didn't want to take me away from him. A couple of years later, the Peterson woman passed, and Bobby came to live with us after that."

Tank let out a whistle. "My goodness, a regular Peyton Place. Grace Metalious could have gotten a few tips from your family."

Peggy chuckled, "Yeah, it is quite a story,"

"You know," Tank said, "I always thought it was weird that you and Bobby both became archaeologists. What got you into it?"

"I liked digging things up as a kid. When I was seven, I found out our neighbor's cat had died five years earlier. I dug it up to see what it looked like. It fascinated me. I started asking for books on animals from Africa: elephants, lions, tigers and such. I read everything I could about the people of Africa and their ancestry. My parents thought I was crazy.

"I thought about majoring in Paleontology but decided on archaeology. Bobby loved the idea and joined me at the University of Arizona after he graduated high school a year later. They have a great program there, so the rest is history," Peggy said with a smile.

"You dug up your neighbor's cat? That's sick," Tank said, wrinkling his nose.

Peggy laughed. "Yeah, maybe. But it was fascinating for me, even at that age."

"Speaking of strange things," Tank said, his tone shifting, "Why do you think Susan went to Berkeley yesterday?"

Peggy blinked, caught off guard by the change in topic. "Wow, nice curveball, Koufax. Where'd that come from?"

Tank shrugged. "Think about it. She could've just called Reardon to ask for help. She didn't need to go all the way to Berkeley. And what do you know about Sandy Kofax?"

"Typical male. Are you suggesting she went there on the outside chance of seeing Wes? She doesn't give two shits about him anymore, and you'd have to live under a rock not to know about the great Kofax," Peggy replied curtly.

"Whatever. Hey, I thought you liked Wes."

"I do. I mean, I did. I thought Wes was a good guy until that thing with Jennifer. The man couldn't keep his Johnson in his pants. What a dickhead."

"Yeah, that was a mess. But Wes regrets it, you know. I talked to him a while back. He's still sick over what he did."

Peggy huffed. "Men. Letting their downstairs brain make all the decisions. Typical."

"And you don't think women do that – Mrs. Peterson, I mean Peggy," Tank said sarcastically.

"Ouch. Well, I deserved that, I guess," Peggy said, frowning.

The two continued to walk, and then Tank had another thought. He turned his head and was about to add a comment over his shoulder when he tripped, falling face-first into the dirt. "Damn it!" he cursed as he scrambled to his knees.

"Are you okay?" Peggy asked, stifling a giggle.

"Yeah, I'm fine, but—oh God," Tank said, his voice trailing off as he glanced down. "What the hell is that?"

Peggy's gaze followed his, and her hands flew to her mouth in horror. "Oh shit. That's disgusting. What did that—a grizzly or something?"

Lying half in half out of the bushes was the half-eaten carcass of a mountain lion—or what was left of it.

"Not a grizzly," Tank said, wiping his hands on his pants as he stood. "There haven't been grizzlies in this area for a century. Maybe a black bear, another mountain lion...or a pack of coyotes."

"Whatever did this didn't just eat it—it shredded it," Peggy pointed out, her voice tight with fear.

Tank squinted down the path, noticing a trail of blood leading away. "Looks like something dragged part of it that way. Should we check it out?"

"Are you nuts? I'm not following it anywhere. What if we run into the thing that did this? I've got a small hunting knife. What do you have?"

"Same. Maybe right. Let's go back and get the others. We'll grab a couple of the shotguns and come back." "Yeah, good idea. You get the others and your guns and come back. While you're gone, I'll stay behind and make sure the camp is safe," Peggy offered with no apology.

Tank opened his mouth to respond when a deafening roar exploded through the forest. The sound was so powerful it seemed to shake the ground beneath them.

"What the hell?" Peggy shrieked as she almost jumped into Tank's arms.

"It came from back there," Tank said, glancing over his shoulder. His voice was tight, his eyes wide. "We need to move. Now."

"I'll be crawling up your ass if you don't run faster than me! GO!" Peggy screamed.

A loud crash followed the roar like trees being ripped from their roots. Neither of them looked back.

The two raced through the forest, dodging branches and stumbling over rocks. Their breath came in ragged gasps, visible in the cold air. Peggy's heart pounded in her chest, each beat echoing the terror coursing through her veins.

Tank slipped on loose gravel, his body crashing into a boulder. He groaned, blood trickling down his face from a gash on his cheek. The roar came again, louder, closer. The thunderous sound violated every reserved human emotion the two retained. In a simultaneous eruption, Tank and Peggy let out a scream neither thought they could make.

"Come on!" Peggy screamed, grabbing his arm and pulling him to his feet.

They scrambled up a steep incline, but Peggy's backpack got caught on a branch, jerking her backward.

"Tank, help. I'm stuck," Peggy cried out.

Howard glanced back and saw his friend in a panic. He slid down to her side and tried to free the pack, but the odd position she was in, and the angle of the hill prevented them from getting it loose.

"Screw it," Peggy shouted, slipping her arms out of the straps, leaving the bag dangling on the branch.

At the top of the hill, Tank turned to help Peggy over the last few feet and happened to glance back—his face drained of color. A dark stain spread across the front of his pants.

Peggy noticed and looked up at him, her fear amplifying as she caught the terror in his eyes. "What? What is it?"

"Don't look back, Peg," Tank stammered. "For the love of God—RUN!"

Without question, Peggy obeyed, head down, legs pumping with everything she had left.

The pair didn't know where they were going. They didn't care as long as it led them to safety. But the trail ended abruptly, blocked by a solid wall of granite.

"There's nowhere to go," Tank gasped, panicking.

"Do you think we can climb!" Peggy said, rushing to the rock wall.

"Are you crazy? There's no way," Tank snapped as he watched her scramble. "This thing goes straight up at least forty feet. There's no way we can climb up."

Peggy ignored Tank, but she gave up after several failed attempts to find footing and handholds.

"Look!" she shouted, dashing toward a small gap between the granite and the shrubs. "Maybe we can hide!"

Peggy pawed at the bushes to get by. Surprisingly, the strands of foliage moved aside like a curtain. Momentarily stunned by what was happening, she slowed only to be pushed from behind by Tank.

"GO, GO, GO," he said in a panic. "It's coming up the slope."

They squeezed through the gap, sliding into an inky void of darkness. The smell hit them immediately—a rancid stench that made Peggy gag.

"Christ," she choked, covering her nose with her shirt. "What is that smell?"

"Something dead," Tank muttered, pulling a flashlight from his belt. He flicked it on, and the beam revealed a gruesome sight.

"Those are human bones?" Peggy gasped, her voice trembling.

"Yes," Tank said grimly. "A lot of them."

"Is that what's smelling so bad?" Peggy pleaded.

"Not sure, but I don't think so," Tank said. "There's no flesh left on any of them, and the bones wouldn't give off that kind of odor."

Suddenly, a low growl rumbled from the darkness behind them. Tank swung the flashlight around, revealing the figure of a man—an Indian in ceremonial feathers and deerskin, standing just inside the entrance.

"Look," Tank stammered. "I don't know why you're here, but we've got to find a hiding place. There's a monster outside. Did you see it? You must have; it was just down the trail."

"You have come as I have prophesized," the man said in perfect English.

Tank kept the light on the man but looked to where Peggy stood. "Do you know this guy?"

"Are you kidding?" she hissed back. "Of course not."

The man's eyes gleamed in the darkness. "We know you, Devon Howard, great-grandson of Deacon Howard. And you, Peggy Tucker, great-granddaughter of David Tucker. One hundred years ago, your ancestors massacred my people. Now, the last of the killers' bloodlines will die."

"What the hell are you talking about?" Peggy shouted, panic rising in her chest. "We haven't done anything to you!"

The man didn't respond.

"Listen, my friend and I only want to get out of here. Please, do you know..." Suddenly, a fire burst to life in the corner of the cave, illuminating two figures lying beside it—a woman and a child. They appeared to be either asleep or dead. "Hello?" Peggy called out, stepping toward them with caution. "Are you okay?"

The two women bolted upright, their eyes wide and blank, and began to scream. The sound was inhuman in its intensity. As they wailed, their clothes started to tear apart as if slashed by invisible blades. Blood gushed from gashes that opened on their skin, pouring down their bodies in a horrifying spectacle.

"Peggy stumbled backward. "What in God's name?" she cried.

Tank turned to the man—but he was gone. In his place stood a monstrous figure, towering over them, its eyes glowing red, its mouth open with rows of jagged teeth. Tank's knees buckled, and he collapsed, weeping uncontrollably.

Peggy Tifton, a well-educated woman who had traveled the world and seen much of man's worst, whirled around to see what happened. She let out a shriek and then fainted in terror, her bowels loosening as her body crumpled into a pile.

CHAPTER 17

Who has a Temper?

Susan and Wes drove for about thirty minutes to Capetown, the Indian's eerie appearance still lingering in their minds, though neither spoke of it. Instead, their conversation turned to more practical matters.

"I'm going to stop by the local police station and see if there's any news about Tank and Peggy before we head to Orca," Susan said, her voice tight with purpose.

"Sounds good," Wes agreed, keeping his eyes on the road ahead.

"I doubt they've done anything," she continued, frustration creeping in. "They all seem like dolts, but it's worth checking out. And let me do the talking. I don't need you losing your temper and getting us thrown in jail. Got it?"

Wes shot her a side glance, genuinely surprised. "Sure, but since when do I have a temper?"

Susan only raised an eyebrow, pulling the car into the police station parking lot.

As they stepped out, Wes scanned the squat, cement block building. "This place looks like it came out of a John Wayne war movie. The walls are probably two feet thick, and every window has bars. What were they afraid of when they built this?"

Susan sighed. "Beats me. Come on, let's get this over with."

Once inside, just as she suspected, the police had no updates and still refused to go to Orca or search for her missing team members. Susan expected this result. She thanked the clerk at the front desk and turned to leave when a door down the hall creaked open, and Chief Daniel Hurley waddled out of his office.

At five-foot-ten and tipping the scales at well over three hundred pounds, Hurley had a smug, self-satisfied air. His round face beamed with a condescending grin. "Ms. Blake," he greeted in a syrupy tone, "asking about your people again, I see."

Susan's eyes narrowed, but she didn't respond.

"You know, if it were up to me, we'd gladly investigate their disappearance," Hurley continued, his grin widening. "But as I told you last time, I don't have the authority to poke around Orca. Besides," he added with a chuckle that jiggled his entire frame, "you and your grave robbers have stirred up a hornet's nest. Guess you'll have to pull the stingers out yourselves."

His laugh reverberated through the small station, making Susan's skin crawl. His words, dripping with mockery, hit her like a slap. Something inside her snapped.

Without thinking, she marched up to him, mere inches from his bloated belly.

"First of all, you pompous mound of cow shit," she snapped, her voice sharp and biting. "Hornets don't leave their stingers behind. So, congratulations on making a complete fool of yourself for that stupid statement."

The color drained from Hurley's face, but Susan kept up the barrage before he could react.

"Secondly," she continued, her tone deadly, "my team was asked by the Smithsonian to investigate Orca. We're not some random treasure hunters tearing up your countryside. The fact that you refuse to help tells me one of two things: either you know something you're not telling us, or you're just too much of a coward to go. Regardless, you and your band of merry idiots are useless."

Hurley's jowls quivered, his face turning beet red. He opened his mouth to shout, but Wes stepped in, sensing the storm about to explode.

"Officer Hurley," Wes said smoothly, stepping between the two combatants and placing a calming hand on Susan's arm. "We understand you're in a difficult position. We appreciate your time."

With a firm but gentle grip, Wes steered Susan toward the door. Susan shot one last venomous glare at the police chief as Wes guided her outside. Once back in the car, Wes buckled up, trying to stifle the grin creeping across his face.

As they pulled onto the road, he couldn't resist anymore. "Sorry for losing my temper in there. I apparently have a problem. Wait, no, that was you."

"Shut up," Susan barked, still seething.

"Well, that was about as close to us landing in jail as that time in Maine. Except I got us out of a likely jam. I'd say we're even now."

Susan's head whipped around, her eyes blazing. "Even? Even? Not by a long shot."

CHAPTER 18

No One Left Behind

By mid-1956, Susan and Wes had been dating for over two years. Their relationship blossomed not only due to their natural chemistry but also their shared passion for archaeology. Wes was more experienced, but Susan quickly made a name for herself—especially after her work with Louis and Mary Leakey at Olduvai Gorge in Tanzania.

The Leakey team had made groundbreaking discoveries in human evolution, including the unearthing of hominids millions of years old—such as Homo habilis and Homo erectus. They had discovered the first Proconsul skull, an extinct ape believed to be ancestral to humans. Later, they unearthed the robust Zinjanthropus skull, also known as Paranthropus boisei.

Although Susan had only been an assistant on the dig, she had helped excavate these significant finds. By association, her reputation grew within paleontology circles.

So, when the opportunity arose to join the Leakey's at a site near Moosehead Lake in Maine, Susan jumped at the chance, and Wes joined her.

One evening, after a dozen long days at the dig site, the crew decided to blow off some steam in the nearby town of Greenville. Alongside Susan and Wes were their assistants:

Perry Cummings, Avery Jennings, and Mary Stewart. They all piled into the Moosehead Pub with the simple goal of enjoying a few beers, eating a hot meal that wasn't cooked by Avery—their self-appointed chef—and having a good time.

Everything was going smoothly. The group relaxed, laughed, and felt the weight of the heavy workload ease away. Then, Benny Tifton and Sid Adams, two locals with a reputation for causing trouble, decided to crash their evening.

Benny made the first move, Sid following him like a loyal shadow. Tifton slid up behind Mary Stewart, placing his hands on her shoulders as if he had a right to be there.

"You're too pretty to be with these guys," Benny whispered into Mary's ear, his breath heavy with the smell of alcohol.

Mary stiffened. "Please take your hands off me," she said, her tone cold but controlled.

"I will," Benny smirked, "but only if you promise to have a drink with me and my buddies. Ditch these losers. You too, sweetheart," he added, glancing over at Susan with a lascivious smile.

That's when Wes stood up.

"I suggest you let go and walk back to your friends," he said, his voice calm but firm. "And I'd do it now if I were you."

Benny scoffed, not backing down. "Well, well, a tough guy? Gonna be a hero, huh? Not a great idea," he sneered, his bravado bolstered by the alcohol coursing through his veins.

Wes didn't flinch. "I won't ask again."

Before Benny could respond, Sid, always the opportunist, aimed a sucker punch at his back. Adams had been Benny's sidekick since their days in elementary school. He wasn't an accomplished fighter, but he was scrappy and knew how to stir up trouble, especially when Benny was around to handle the heavy lifting. Sid's usual strategy was to start a fight with his mouth, then let Benny finish it with his fists.

Wes caught the movement out of the corner of his eye and dodged, Sid's blow glanced off his hip instead of landing squarely. Wes dropped to one knee but quickly sprang back up. Adams stumbled back, surprised by Wes's speed and due to the fact the man was at least a foot taller.

Benny knew the drill and immediately lunged at Perry Cummings, seated at the booth's end. Perry, soft-spoken and unassuming, didn't look like much of a threat. He was thin, balding prematurely at thirty-three, and wore round wirerimmed glasses. But Perry was far from helpless. He grabbed his heavy beer mug and smashed it into Benny's forehead with a loud crack. The thug collapsed onto the table, blood pouring from the gash.

Sid, now seeing that his brawler of a friend was out cold on the table, stepped back in disbelief. In a matter of seconds, the entire dynamic had shifted.

"Hey, guys," Susan whispered, her voice edged with panic. She and Mary had backed away from the chaos, but Susan kept scanning the rest of the bar. "Just a heads up — their friends are heading straight for us. This is about to get a lot worse." Avery Jennings, who had been trapped in the booth next to Perry, finally managed to push past and join Wes.

"This is bad," Avery muttered under his breath.

"Yep," Wes agreed, his fists still clenched. "I think we're about to get our asses kicked."

Still shaken by his sudden shift from bystander to combatant, Perry whispered, "Guys, there's an exit door down the hall behind Mary and Susan. Maybe we should make a run for it."

"We wouldn't get far," Wes replied, scanning the room. "They'd be on us before we could get everyone out."

Five men gathered around Sid, all looking eager to finish what had been started.

"Gentlemen let's not do anything crazy," Susan said, stepping in front of Wes and the others. "We don't need this to escalate to where someone goes to jail, or worse, to the hospital. So, can we all calm down."

But before things could worsen, a booming voice cut through the noise. "I think jail is the least of your worries, little lady," Sheriff Amos Thompson bellowed.

The officer, a tall, imposing figure, pushed through the crowd, his eyes landing on Wes.

"What's your name, son?" the sheriff asked, his question dripping with authority.

"Wes. Wes Cravenfish," Wes answered, still on edge.

The men behind the sheriff erupted into laughter, Thompson included.

"Craven what?" he scoffed, his face contorting into an exaggerated expression of disbelief.

"Cravenfish," Wes repeated, standing his ground.

"Well, Mr. Cravenfish," the sheriff said, his tone shifting. "That boy you just laid out happens to be my nephew. So, here's how this is gonna go: either you turn around, and I'll cuff you and take you in, or..." His gaze slid over to Susan, lingering a little too long. "Or I let these boys show you some real Greenville hospitality."

Feeling the sheriff's eyes crawl over her, Susan clenched her fists. She had half a mind to grab a knife and throw it at his head. Sensing her friends rising fury, Mary stepped in front of Susan.

"Officer," Mary said with an icy calm, "that man," she gestured to Benny, still bleeding on the table, "he grabbed me and wouldn't let go. We asked him to stop. He didn't. Then that punk sucker punched my friend in the back, and while that was happening, the other one dove at my other friend." Mary conveniently left out how Benny ended up face-first on the table, blood spilling from his head.

"Huh. Is that what happened?" the sheriff asked, his eyes narrowing as he looked at his fellow townsmen.

The men mumbled and shuffled uncomfortably. Sid, however, wasn't backing down. "Sheriff, me and Benny were just having a friendly chat with the ladies. Their boyfriend got jealous, stood up, and got in Benny's face. I knew he would throw a punch, so I stepped in to help. But before I could do act, they did that to Benny."

As if on cue, Benny moaned, still semi-conscious.

"That's a bald-faced lie," Susan scoffed. "They started this whole thing by that jackass putting his hands where they didn't belong. And that punk threw the first punch. No one from our side did anything."

"Yes, you would say that. Whatever it takes to keep your boy out of jail. I get it. Nice try. Except our guy is the one laid out and bleeding."

Sheriff Thompson retrieved his handcuffs with deliberate slowness. "Now, turn around," he ordered, gesturing to Wes. "You guys take Benny to Doc Baker's, get him stitched up, and then take him straight home. I'll take this boy to the jail."

"Where might that be?" Susan demanded, her frustration clear.

"Go out the door, turn left, walk two blocks, and turn left again. Can't miss it. Visiting hours start at ten a.m. tomorrow morning."

"You're kidding me, right? That's ridiculous!" Susan protested.

Thompson stared at Susan, his eyes scanning her from head to toe. "I tell you what," he drawled. "Come to the station in an hour. It'll give me time to book your friend. After that, you can bail him out."

"And how much is that going to cost me?" Susan asked, arms crossed, her glare sharp.

The men standing around the sheriff began to laugh and snicker.

"Our normal fee. Three hundred dollars," the sheriff said with a smirk.

"Three hundred dollars? That's outrageous!" Avery barked, incredulous.

"Like I said. You come and see me in an hour, and we'll talk it out. Maybe we can discuss a middle ground. Now, pay your bill and get out," he grumbled, grabbing Wes by the arm and steering him roughly toward the door.

Once the sheriff and Wes had left, Perry spoke up, his voice laced with concern. "Susan, that sheriff is trouble. It's damn clear what he has in mind. We'll all go with you when you head back."

"Yeah, no way you're going in alone," Mary agreed, frowning. "By the way, do you even have three hundred dollars?"

Susan sighed. "No, I've got about ninety. How much do you guys have?"

Avery rifled through his wallet, counting his money with a grimace. "I've got ninety-three."

"I've got sixty," Mary said, adding her share.

The group turned to Perry, who grimaced and said, "Um, only twenty."

Mary huffed. "Now what? We've only got two hundred and sixty-three dollars, and we still haven't paid our tab here, which is another thirty-three bucks."

Susan's eyes lit up as she snapped her fingers. "Wait, I've got my checkbook in the car. Maybe the sheriff will take a check."

"You'd better hope so," Mary said, her voice low. "Or who knows how long they'll keep Wes locked up."

"And what they might do to him while he's there," Perry added with obvious concern.

Fifty minutes later, Susan, Mary, Avery, and Perry arrived at the police station. Deputy Ronald Perkins sat behind the front desk, his feet up and a smug grin plastered across his face.

"Can I help you folks?" he asked, not looking up from a magazine.

"We're here to bail out Wes Cravenfish," Susan said, her voice clipped and to the point.

The deputy snorted, then burst into uncontrollable laughter. "Cravenfish? Man, that still cracks me up! What kind of dumbass name is that? Cravenfish. Dang, if that ain't the stupidest name I've ever heard."

Susan's patience was wearing thin. "Yeah, yeah, it's dumb. Can we bail him out now, please?"

The deputy wiped unseen tears from his eyes, still chuckling. "Well, here's the thing. The sheriff made it real clear—only you can bail him out." He leaned back in his chair, the grin on his face like a cat that had swallowed a canary. "Said to bring the tall, pretty one to his office when you got here."

Susan's companions started protesting, their voices rising in a chorus of disbelief. But the deputy remained unfazed, his smile never faltering.

"Okay, okay," Susan said, raising her hands to quiet the group. "We can't leave Wes in there any longer. I'll handle this. Deputy, let's go."

"Susan, no!" Mary stepped forward; her face full of concern.

"I can take care of myself," Susan assured her. "I'll be fine."

The deputy led Susan down a short hallway to the sheriff's office, the click of her boots echoing off the linoleum floor. A brass plaque reading Sheriff Thompson hung prominently on the door. "This way, ma'am. The sheriff's been waiting for you."

I bet he has; she thought as dread seeped into her veins. The deputy ushered her inside and closed the door as he left.

The office was far from what she had expected. It looked more like a CEO's private den than a small-town sheriff's workspace. The walls were lined with rich walnut wood paneling, and the ceiling was adorned with intricately carved tiles. A large, ornate desk dominated the room, but what caught her attention most was the oversized leather couch against one wall.

"Not going near that thing," Susan muttered, her distaste palpable.

The sheriff was nowhere in sight, but a door at the back of the office opened, and she heard the unmistakable sound of a toilet flushing. Sheriff Thompson emerged a moment later, adjusting his belt with a wide smile splashed across his face.

"Ah, sorry about that," he said with a wink. "Had to take care of some business." His smirk widened as he leaned back against the desk. "Speaking of business, I'm guessing you're here to negotiate."

You are a disgusting, loathing pig of a man, Susan wanted to say. She straightened; her face set in hard lines. "I'm here to bail out Mr. Cravenfish. Three hundred dollars is ridiculous, but I'll pay it."

She reached into her purse, but the sheriff held up a hand before she could pull out her checkbook, his grin growing even more suggestive. "Now, now, I'm not unreasonable. If you think the price is too high, I'm sure we can find a way to… make it less." He reclined on the couch, legs spread wide, his eyes gleaming with predatory intent.

Another stomach flip-flop, but she refused to flinch. "Look, sheriff, I don't know what you're insinuating, but if it involves anything other than me writing you a check, you're sorely mistaken."

Thompson's smirk widened, and he made no effort to hide a glance toward his crotch, where a bulge was forming. "As I said, I'm not unreasonable. If you don't want to pay the full amount, I'd be more than willing to accept… less – cash." Susan's eyes narrowed, her voice cutting and razor-sharp. "Here's what's going to happen. I'm writing you a check for two hundred and fifty dollars—not three hundred. Then you're going to release my friend from this lousy excuse for a jail. If you don't, I'll have my good friend, Dr. Mary Leakey, call Louise Conkrite—yes, Walter's wife—and let her know exactly how you run things around here."

"I'm betting your constituents wouldn't be too thrilled when a CBS news team shows up and exposes you for what you are and what you do here. So, if you don't want that to happen, get your ass up and take the check now."

The sheriff's face drained of color. His cocky posture faltered, and he crossed his legs awkwardly. His eyes darted to Susan, trying to gauge if she was bluffing.

"You expect me to believe you know those people?" he challenged, but his voice had lost some of its bravado. "Why shouldn't I just lock you up next to your boyfriend? Then I don't have to worry about anything."

"Go ahead," Susan said, folding her arms in defiance. "But when we don't show up at the dig site tomorrow, the Leakey's will come looking. And when they do, are you planning to ask Mrs. Leakey for a blow job, too? I'm sure that would really enhance your career prospects in law enforcement."

The sheriff's mouth tightened into a thin line, his hands balling into fists at his sides. For several long, tense moments, they stared each other down.

Finally, with a growl of frustration, he snapped, "Just give me the damn three hundred dollars."

"It's two-fifty, and you're lucky I'm giving you that." Before Thompson could object, Susan filled out the check, handed it to the Sheriff, and walked to the door. "Shall we?"

CHAPTER 19

The Crash

"So, like I said, now we're even?" Wes quipped with a cheeky grin.

"Even? HAH! Hardly," Susan scoffed. "If you remember correctly, keeping you out of jail cost me three hundred bucks."

"Two-fifty," Wes corrected with a smirk.

"And I almost had to 'service' the constable with more than just the money, if you recall," she snapped. "That pervert's probably still looking for us. So, no, we're nowhere near even. JERK!"

Wes couldn't help but laugh, though Susan wasn't amused. "I still can't believe you got away with that whole story about Mary and Conkrite's wife. The woman didn't even know his wife, did she?"

"Beats me," Susan said, her lips curling into a faint smile. "But we're damn lucky that doofus sheriff believed it. Otherwise, we'd be 'missing persons' in that town, never to be seen again."

Wes was smiling, and then his face softened. "You know that time in Maine was almost two years to the day of our first date."

"What? What are you talking about? It wasn't... was it?" Susan's voice lowered; her tone thoughtful as she mentally retraced the timeline.

"You don't have to think too hard about it," Wes replied, clearly enjoying the trip down memory lane. "Our first official date was at McClenaghan's in El Paso. It was in May of 1956, and you were celebrating your first dig since graduation with some of your co-workers. I happened to be there with Kent Spillman, your foreman on that site."

Susan smiled, the memory coming back. "You were there with Kent? That's right."

"You guys were at the bar, and Kent and I were having dinner in the dining room. I went to the bathroom and saw you sitting there. We locked eyes—for only a few seconds, but the moment jolted me. When I got back to my table, I told Spillman I'd fallen in love."

Susan rolled her eyes, but there was a gentleness to her expression.

"He laughed at me and said, 'What, with yourself, in the bathroom?' I'll never forget his words. I said, 'Nope, with the beautiful brunette at the bar.' He got up to check and came back saying, 'You mean Susan Blake? Come on, I'll introduce you. I had no idea he knew you—purely coincidental."

"Okay, fine, but that wasn't a date," Susan countered. "That doesn't count."

"No, it doesn't," Wes admitted. "But three days later, I came to your site and flashed my Smithsonian Institute ID card. You couldn't resist me after that. You were a big fan of the Institute, and since I was working in their archaeology division, I asked you out right then and there. That Friday night, May second, 1956, we went to McClenaghan's alone, and—well, the rest was history."

Susan's expression relaxed momentarily, but then her hands tightened on the steering wheel. "Okay, you got part of that right. Yes, I loved the Smithsonian, and that's probably why I even entertained the idea of going out with you. So, I'll give you credit for that. But let's be clear—I wasn't drooling over you at the site, that's for sure."

Wes grinned, unfazed. "Matter of opinion. But after dinner, when you came to my hotel? That sealed the deal. We were inseparable after that."

There was a momentary flicker of light in Susan's eyes, a glimmer of the affection they'd once shared. But then her expression darkened, and her eyes hardened.

"Yeah, Wes, the first time was wonderful," she said, her voice sharp. "A lot of nights after that were great, too. We were a match made in heaven—or so I thought. I was ready to be Mrs. Cravenfish, to have your babies—that is, until you screwed Jennifer on my couch."

Wes flinched at the bluntness of her words, the guilt striking him like a blow to the gut. "I wish you wouldn't keep bringing that up," he said in a whisper, his tone heavy with remorse.

Susan's glare could have burned through steel. "Yeah, well, I deserved better."

Wes sighed, knowing there was no arguing with her on this point. After a few moments of silence, he ventured cautiously, "You… you wanted to have my kids?"

A tear slipped down Susan's cheek, her face tense with the weight of old wounds. She didn't speak for several seconds, and when she did, her voice wavered between pain and frustration. "Damn it, Wes, don't you get it? I was in love with you. I dreamed of being Mrs. Cravenfish. I wanted a house full of little Cravenfish kids running around. Although, to be honest," she added with a small, bitter laugh, "I might've fought to keep my name and had the kids go by 'Blake.' Let's face it— 'Cravenfish'? They'd have been bullied forever."

Wes let out a chuckle, though his heart ached. "Don't I know it?"

The two sat silent for a few moments until Wes broke the momentary silence. "Susan, you must know that I wanted those things too. A home, kids, a life with you... you, most of all. I will never stop hating myself for messing it up. I'm so sorry. If there was any way to go back and what I did, you know that I would."

Susan sighed, the anger still simmering beneath her calm tone. "I know, Wes. But what's done is done."

Quiet filled the car again for a few more miles, the tension hanging thick in the air. Then, out of nowhere, Wes barked, "Holy shit!"

Susan slammed on the brakes, glancing in the rearview mirror. "What? Did I miss the road?"

"No, but something just clicked," Wes said, his voice rising. "Why didn't I think of it before? The Capetown police chief's last name—Hurley."

"Hurley?" Susan said, frowning. "What about it?"

Wes's eyes widened. "It's Hurley. Daniel Hurley. The same last name as three of the people we talked about. Doesn't that seem like more than just a coincidence?"

Susan's frown deepened. "I guess... but 'Hurley' isn't exactly an uncommon name. Besides, those deaths were decades ago. Could he be related?"

Wes shrugged. "I don't know. But it's possible, isn't it? And remember all the other names from the massacre that went missing. Not to mention the man's weird demeanor about helping. I could be totally wrong here, but I'm sensing a connection."

Susan shook her head, her focus returning to the road ahead. "Possibly. But right now, we have to find our friends. Look—is that the turn for Orca?"

Wes squinted, leaning forward. "Yeah, that's it."

Susan turned onto the rough, uneven path leading to the ruins of Orca. But even as she navigated the bumpy terrain, her thoughts were racing, the possible relationship between Chief Hurley and the missing people gnawing at her. Her foot pressed harder on the gas than she realized.

"You might want to slow down," Wes suggested, his voice cautious. "I know your mind is in an uproar, but this isn't exactly a highway. We don't want to kill ourselves before we figure out what's going on."

Susan shot him a sharp glance. The last time she'd looked at him like that, she was tossing his clothes off her apartment balcony. Wisely, Wes raised his hands in mock surrender and dropped the subject.

But just as Susan turned her attention back to the road, she screamed.

Three people—a man, a woman, and a child—stood in the middle of the road, directly in their way.

"WATCH IT!" Wes shouted.

Susan yanked the steering wheel to the left, narrowly missing the figures, but she overcorrected. The car veered wildly, fishtailing on the uneven ground. She tried desperately to regain control, but it was no use. The vehicle sideswiped one tree before slamming head-on into another.

The impact wasn't at a high speed—around twenty miles per hour—but it felt like they'd hit a brick wall doing one hundred. Susan had been wearing her seatbelt, but the lap restraint did little to stop her head from smashing into the steering wheel. The collision produced a one-inch gash right below her hairline and next to the bruise she had gotten earlier.

Her passenger, however, was not wearing his safety belt. Cravenfish rocketed forward upon the car's collision with the tree. His body struck the dash, the windshield, and the car's roof all at once, with his head taking the brunt of the crash.

Several long moments passed after the accident, with neither Susan nor Wes moving. The accident had left them both stunned.

Susan groaned, her head spinning. She blinked multiple times, trying to remember what had happened. A stream of blood trickled down her forehead, along her nose, and over her cheek. At first, she didn't even register it—her mind still foggy. But when the blood flowed into her right eye, panic set in.

Rubbing furiously at the sticky fluid, she gritted her teeth in frustration. Using her blouse, she wiped her face and eyes, clearing her vision.

After taking a deep breath, she turned to check on Wes. "Wes, are you alright? WES!" The man was unresponsive. A large welt had already formed on his forehead, and a small cut marred his left cheek.

"WES!" Susan shouted. She unbuckled her seat belt, slid over, and gave the man a slight shake. "Wes, please. Come on, wake up," she pleaded. The man began to stir. "Oh, thank God. Wes, Honey, are you alright?"

After a brief hesitation, Cravenfish groaned, "Honey? Did you just call me Honey?"

Susan let out a half-laugh, half-sigh of relief. "That you heard?" she said, grimacing. "Are you hurt? Anything broken?"

"Not sure… Maybe my head," he muttered, his hand moving to his cheek. "Ouch. Apparently, I hurt my face, too." He winced as he touched the cut. He gingerly pressed on the welt on his forehead. "Double ouch."

His eyes fluttered open, blinking as he tried to focus. When he was able to focus on Susan, he gasped. "SUSAN! What the hell? Are you okay?"

"I'm fine. Just hit my head on the steering wheel. Looks worse than it is. Think you can walk?"

"I don't know. I think so. Can you come around and help me out?"

Susan nodded and climbed out of the driver's seat, hurrying to the passenger side. She opened the door, and Wes slowly swung his legs out, staying seated on the edge of the seat for a moment.

"I'm a bit woozy," he admitted. "Give me a second."

Susan looked back at the road. Her voice was quiet, shaken. "Did you see what I saw?"

Wes let out a heavy sigh. "Thank God. I thought I was losing it again. Yeah, I saw them. Three Indians—a man, a woman, and a girl, I think. And… the man looked familiar. I think he was the one at the gas station."

"That's not possible? We're at least twenty miles from there. How could he have gotten here so fast?"

"Yeah, you're right," Wes agreed, rubbing his temples.

"And where are they now? Though I didn't feel us hit anything, well, not until those two trees, there was no way I could have missed them. But there are no bodies on the road. How is that possible?"

"I can't even imagine," Wes replied, his voice strained.

"Wes, the bridge isn't far. From there, we must walk about a quarter of a mile to our camp. We better get to the others as soon as we can. I don't know what's happening here, but we need to move. Think you can make it?"

"I think so. Help me up," Wes grunted as he struggled to stand. With Susan's aid, Cravenfish stood. At first, he was a little shaky, but he soon got his bearings and began to feel more alert. "Nothing feels broken. I think I'm good."

"Thank God. Let's grab what gear we can carry and go to the camp. We need to find out what's going on. You sure you're okay?" Susan asked.

"Yeah. I think other than the golf ball-sized bump on my head and the small cut on my cheek, I'm okay," Cravenfish answered. "How about we discuss that whole "Babe" comment during our stroll."

"I didn't say babe, I said Honey."

"Aha! I knew I heard it," Wes exclaimed in satisfaction, though he winced in pain from the effort.

Susan shook her head, dismissing the conversation, and the two of them gathered what they could carry. When they neared the bridge, Susan's eyes locked on something in the distance.

"Uh oh," she said under her breath.

Wes looked over at her. "Uh oh? What, uh oh?"

Susan pointed toward a car parked near the others. "Rudy. That's his car."

"Great, just great. Did you know he was going to be here?"

"Of course not. Why would I need to ask you to come and help if I knew Rudy would be here...Shit, I didn't mean that like it sounded," Susan said.

"Yeah, maybe not, but you said it. Once we get to the camp, you can have somebody drive me back to Capetown. No need to have Rudy mad at you too."

"So, you're mad?"

This time, Cravenfish gave Blake the stare. After a moment of silence between the two, he said, "Look, let's just see what's going on at the camp, then we can decide that Rudy's a jerk. I mean, then we can decide what to do. If your people are back, then I can leave. If not, I wouldn't care if Rudy and his whole family were there. I'm going to find Tank and Peggy."

"Thanks. I really am happy you are here to help."

Wes believed her, and though he appreciated her words, it still hurt. As the two were about to cross the narrow footbridge, Wes noticed something which immediately concerned him. "I hope your team has some spare tires stashed in their gear,"

"What do you mean?" Susan asked.

"Well, if I'm correct, every car here has had a tire slashed," Wes said as he made his way to where they were parked. Working his way around each one, he nodded. "Yep, looks like they used a good-sized hunting knife to puncture a tire on each car."

"Why would anyone do that?" Susan said as she rushed over to inspect the tires.

"Not sure, but if I were to make a guess, I'd say somebody doesn't want us being here. Or..."

"Or what?"

"Or they don't care that you've come, only that they aren't going to let you leave. Either way, we better not waste any more time and go check out the camp," Wes said as he slung his gear on his back and headed toward the bridge.

It took twenty minutes to reach the point where the trees ended, and the open range of the plateau started. From there, Wes and Susan could see Orca's ruins straight ahead and the tents from the archaeologist encampment just to the left of the town.

"I see some movement. Looks like there is some sort of agitation. Are you able to move any faster?" Susan asked.

"I'm fine. Get going," Wes replied as he hefted his gear tighter to his shoulder and began to trot. They made the crossing to the tents within a few minutes. As they entered the camp perimeter, Bobby Peterson rushed toward them.

"Oh, thank God you're back. Rudy's losing it," Bobby said, his voice frantic. Then his eyes widened as he noticed the blood on Susan's face. "What the hell happened to you?"

Before Susan could answer, Bobby's gaze shifted to Wes. "And what's he doing here?"

Susan glanced back at Wes and said, "We had a little car incident, but neither of us was hurt badly. And I asked Wes to come and help, and…"

"And you thought inviting Wes with Rudy here would be a good idea? No offense, Wes, buddy, but Rudy…" Bobby said as Wes jogged up.

Susan shot Bobby a look. "I didn't know Rudy was going to be here. And after you told me Tank and Peggy were missing, I knew Wes would help find them."

Bobby sighed. "Fine. But Rudy's been acting… well, you'll see." He gestured toward the tents. "Tank and Peggy are still missing. And since I spoke to you, Julia has come down with some kind of sickness. Rudy thinks it's malaria. She's been vomiting, has muscle pain, fever, the whole deal."

"I'll check on her," Wes offered, giving Susan a knowing look. "Maybe you can talk to Rudy before he sees me."

And right on cue, Rudy emerged from his tent.

"Oh, thank God you're here, babe," Rudy called out, striding over. His relief quickly turned to alarm. "What happened to your face? Why are you covered in blood?" His eyes narrowed when he saw Wes. "And why the hell is he here?"

"Babe?" Wes muttered with a smirk, glancing at Susan.

"First, I'm ok. Just hit my head on the steering wheel of the car."

"Hit your head on the steering wheel? What are you talking about?" Rudy said as he glowered at Cravenfish.

"Hey, I wasn't driving," Wes said, hands held up in defense.

"Listen, it doesn't matter. I asked him to come. I didn't know you would be here. Reardon wasn't available, and Wes is familiar with the area and the team," Susan said, trying to defend her actions. "And with Tank and Susan missing, I figured we could use his help."

"Babe? No kidding," Wes repeated, his voice louder now, full of mockery. "Didn't take long for ol' Rudy to swoop in and save the day, huh?"

Rudy missed the first time Wes had thrown out the sarcastic "babe" comment, but not this time. His eyes narrowed as he turned toward Susan, and then, in a show of dominance, he grabbed her by the shoulders and pulled her into a kiss. Susan didn't resist, but she didn't exactly reciprocate either. It was a gesture she allowed, more out of habit than affection.

Wes muttered under his breath, "Ah—babe. Super."

CHAPTER 20

Rudy to the Rescue

At thirty-seven, Rudolph "Rudy" Stevens fancied himself an archaeologist despite lacking the formal degree others in the field earned. Rudy had inherited his family's vast oil fields in Texas after his parents died in a car accident in '51. But the corporate world never suited him, and after a brief and uneventful run as CEO, he sold his holdings to Standard Oil in 1953, becoming a millionaire many times over.

With his newfound fortune, Stevens began globe-trotting, using his wealth to gain favor and secure spots on various archaeological expeditions. He first crossed paths with Susan and Wes at a dig in 1956—an ancient Paleo-Indian site near the Mississippi River in Missouri.

Rudy claimed Native American ancestry, yet his proof was as thin as his archaeological qualifications. His family hailed from northern California, an area with several tribal groups, but he could never substantiate legitimate ties. However, this fact never stopped him from waxing poetic about his "heritage" whenever the opportunity arose.

Susan and Wes had initially approached Stevens for funding for their Missouri expedition. He was only scheduled to visit the camp for a couple of days to assess the project, but after meeting Susan, Rudy became enamored and extended his stay, determined to win her over.

One afternoon, Rudy found Susan alone, brushing dirt from a clay pot she had uncovered. He decided the time was right for his move.

"Susan," Rudy began, his tone wavering as he worked beside her, "I'm glad we've got a moment together to talk. There's something I've been meaning to tell you."

Susan didn't look up from her work. "What is it, Rudy?" Her voice was distant, absorbed in the task at hand.

Rudy hesitated, then plunged ahead. "I'm in love with you."

Susan froze mid-brush. Her breath caught as she turned to face him. "What?"

"I know it sounds crazy," Rudy continued, sweat beading on his sunbaked face, "but I've never felt this way with anyone. I just—" Before Susan could react, Rudy leaned in and kissed her.

Susan recoiled, yanking herself away. "Rudy, you're lucky I don't punch you in the face! Try that again, and I will."

He stepped back, mortified. "I—I'm sorry, Susan. I couldn't help myself." He dabbed at his forehead with a rag, his face flushed red with embarrassment. "Listen, all I'm asking is for you to consider me. I'm a decent guy... and, well, rich too." He gave her a weak smile.

Susan's glare could have melted stone. "You're not in love with me, Rudy. You don't even know me. You're infatuated, maybe. Though I'm not sure why. But that's it. And besides,

you know Wes and I are together. We've been together for three years. And to be certain there are no doubts,
I don't care how much money you have."

"I know, I know," Rudy sighed. "I'm sorry. I shouldn't have kissed you—it may have been a bit premature. But let me say this—someday, you'll need me. When the time comes, I'll be there."

Neither of them noticed Wes watching from a distance. He had been making his way back from a nearby bluff when he caught sight of the kiss. Anger churned in his stomach, but he held back, waiting to see how Susan would respond. Her reaction was apparent, which eased his tension—though not entirely.

Wes marched over, closing the gap in long strides. "What the hell do you think you are doing?" he demanded, his face inches from Rudy's. "You think hitting on Susan is smart? I guarantee it's not."

Rudy backed up; hands raised in surrender. "I made a mistake, okay? I'm sorry. It won't happen again." Sweat dripped down his forehead as the desert sun baked him and the landscape, making Rudy look like a guilty schoolboy caught in the act. "Listen. Let's forget this ever happened. I'll pack up and leave first thing in the morning. And don't worry, you'll still get your funding. I promise."

This episode might have ended Rudy's interest in Susan—if not for Wes's colossal blunder with Susan's roommate, Jennifer. It was a betrayal Susan couldn't forgive. Sensing his opportunity, Rudy swooped back in, comforting Susan during her heartbreak.

When Wes found out Susan was spending time with Rudy, he was devastated. He had made a terrible mistake with Jennifer, but he still loved Susan. Seeing her turn to Rudy soon after their split pushed Wes into despair.

He packed up and left, taking a job at the University of California, Berkeley. But the pain lingered. Wes began drinking more and drifting from dig to dig, woman to woman, never quite able to settle. It was a formula for disaster, proven when the university fired him for his dalliance with Pablo Estefan's daughter.

CHAPTER 21

Rudy Steps Out

"Susan, we've got to get out of here," Rudy said, his voice shaky. "Something unnatural is stalking us."

Susan raised an eyebrow. "What do you mean, unnatural?"

"A beast. Huge. At least I think it's huge," Rudy stammered. "Its roar is like a freight train. We found where it crashed through the brush—the destruction was almost eight feet wide and over ten feet high."

Susan turned to Bobby. "Bobby, what's he talking about?"

Bobby nodded. "He's not wrong. The damage is real. I've never seen anything like it."

Susan frowned. "Could it be a pack of animals?"

"Doubt it," Bobby replied. "Besides, nothing I know of can cause destruction four feet above our heads unless a herd of elephants lives here."

Before Susan could respond, Wes emerged from Julia's tent. His expression was grim. "Julia needs a doctor. She's not only sick—she's injured. Her arm's infected. She's barely conscious."

"What?" Bobby's face paled. "I thought she was just feverish. She didn't mention any problems with her arm."

"She told me she found some green, slimy fluid on a tree, almost like mucus. She was collecting a sample when some of it got on a scratch she had on her forearm. The area is now festering. Hadn't anyone been keeping an eye on it?" Wes said, anger clear in his voice.

"Wes, she only mentioned finding the substance yesterday. There's no way it a wound could have gotten septic so fast," Bobby said.

Shaking his head, Wes said, "Regardless, someone needs to take her to Capetown. The rest of us need to gear up and search for Tank and Peggy."

"I'll take—" Rudy began, but when he saw the look Susan shot him, he quickly changed his mind. "On second thought, babe, you go. I'll stay and help look for Tank and Peggy."

Susan crossed her arms. "If you think I'm leaving you and Wes alone to kill each other, you're crazy. Bobby will go with Julia, and I'll stay."

Wes smiled. "Good call, Susan."

Susan gave him the same icy stare she had given Rudy.

Wes looked away. "There is one problem with our plan. Every car in camp has a flat tire."

Rudy's face fell. "A flat tire? What? That's insane. I didn't have a flat when I arrived."

"I think someone deliberately sabotaged the vehicles to trap us here. The good news is they only slashed one tire on each car. If we have spare tires, we can replace one, and Bobby can take Julia to safety. Once they're on their way, we'll start searching for Tank and Peggy."

Before anyone could respond, a bone-rattling roar tore through the air, shaking the trees and sending shockwaves through the camp. Wes felt it reverberate in his chest, like a hammer striking a steel drum.

"Holy mother of God," he breathed. "Was that what you've been hearing?"

"Yep," Susan replied, clinging to Wes's arm. Her grip was tight, her body nearly melding into his. "But this time, it's a lot closer."

Rudy, who had heard the noise before and should have held his ground, took off running toward the trail leading back to the cars, not even looking back to see if Susan was coming or staying.

"Rudy, where are you going? Come back!" Susan shouted.

"Hell no. I don't care if every tire on every car is flat. I'll run back to town if I must," Rudy screamed over his shoulder.

"What about me? What about Tank and Peggy?"

Rudy didn't slow down. "I'll send help!" he called, disappearing into the trees.

Wes smirked, shaking his head. "You sure know how to pick 'em."

"I can't believe this," Susan muttered, her face pale with frustration and fear. She stared after Rudy as if she expected him to realize what he was doing and to turn around for her. But he didn't.

Another roar split the air—closer, angrier. The ground trembled as something massive barreled through the forest, shattering branches and crashing through the underbrush.

"We've got to move," Wes said, snapping into action. "Let's deal with Julia first, then focus on finding Tank and Peggy. Leaving her here isn't an option."

"We could take her to Orca," Bobby suggested, nodding toward the distant ruins. "There are still a few buildings standing. We could hide her there."

"Great idea. Let's rig up a stretcher," Wes said, his tone urgent. "Bobby, grab a cot. We'll make one out of that. Susan, check on Julia and ensure she's ready to move. I'll get my rifle and whatever weapons we've got left."

When Susan entered Julia's tent, there was an odor of rancidity. She covered her nose and mouth with the crook of her arm and walked over to the cot where Julia was lying.

"Julia?" she called as she approached the cot. "Are you awake?"

No response.

Susan's heart pounded as she stepped closer. Julia's back was to her, the thin blanket draped over her still form. Susan reached out, hesitated, then rolled her over.

Julia's eyes were wide open, staring blankly at the ceiling. Her skin was pale, tinged with a sickly hue, and there was no mistaking the rigid stillness of death.

"Oh, Julia," Susan whispered, her voice breaking. She backed away from the cot, the tears stinging her eyes. She turned and stumbled out of the tent, feeling the weight of the situation crash on her all at once.

Outside, she stood frozen, watching Wes and Bobby prepare the gear. She couldn't speak; the words catching in her throat, and instead, she wrapped her arms around herself, trying to hold back the sobs.

Wes noticed her hesitation and rushed over. "Susan, what's wrong?"

She didn't have to say it. Wes saw the answer in her tear-filled eyes.

"Julia's dead isn't she?" he whispered, pulling her into a tight embrace. "I'm so sorry."

Bobby watched the two in anguish. "Oh shit," he muttered under his breath. "I knew this was coming. I knew as soon as they showed up together—poor Rudy didn't stand a chance." He shook his head as he looked away.

Before anyone could process Julia's death, a scream shattered the moment.

"RUN!" A voice shrieked from the edge of the woods, desperate and terrified. "For the love of GOD—RUN!"

Rudy came crashing back through the trees, running faster than when he'd fled. His face was twisted in fear, eyes wide with panic.

"It's a monster! A BIG FUCKING MONSTER!" he screamed. "I saw it tear down the bridge like it was made with a kid's building blocks! It's coming this way!"

It was well over one hundred yards from the trees to the group. Rudy crossed the expanse in record time. But when he got to where they were standing, he kept on going, not saying a word.

"Huh," Susan breathed out as he raced by. "He left me behind again. Unbelievable..."

Wes glanced at Bobby and Susan, his heart hammering. "Grab your guns—now."

CHAPTER 22

Following the Trail

The roar came again, followed by the violent shaking of trees as the creature plowed through the forest, closer than ever. Wes, Susan, and Bobby armed themselves. They stood shoulder to shoulder, their eyes fixed on the tree line, waiting for the beast to emerge.

But nothing came.

"Why isn't it coming?" Susan asked, her voice a choked whisper.

Bobby was as puzzled as the others, until a thought struck him. He tilted his head to the side, glanced up at the sky, and realization dawned. "Uh, guys, I think I just figured something out."

"What is it?" Wes asked as he and Susan lowered their guns.

"The sun, that's what's holding the thing back."

"What do you mean," Susan asked.

"I think it's why it didn't chase Rudy out of the woods. It doesn't like the sunlight. For some reason, I think it affects it. Maybe blinds it. The enormous tree canopies nearly block out the light in the forest, so it's likely safe inside. And we're relatively safe out here. But once the sun goes down, I'm guessing it will emerge from the shadows, and then, well…"

"Yeah, then we're in deep shit," Wes finished.

"I think so. How's Julia? Can she be moved?" Bobby asked with trepidation.

In a trembling voice, Susan said, "Bobby. I'm afraid Julia's Dead."

"What? How's that possible?"

"It must have been the substance she found," Susan said. "Whatever got into the cut on her arm—it poisoned her. I think it's from the creature in those woods."

Wes sighed, glancing at the afternoon's sun. "We've got to move. I hate leaving Julia's body, but we'll be next if we don't locate Tank and Peggy and get out of here. Plus..." Wes said as he glanced to the sky, "We've only got a couple hours of sunlight left.

After the three gathered the rest of what they could carry, including shotguns for Bobby and Susan and Wes' rifle and handgun, Bobby led them toward the path Tank and Peggy had gone.

"They went this way," Bobby said as they walked. "We spent most of our time in town, but Tank decided to scout around to see if he could discover an explanation of what happened to the inhabitants.

"Tank asked Peggy to tag along with him. He told us he discovered some artifacts closer to these woods, and he thought there might be more in other areas of the plateau," Bobby said as he pushed aside some branches to give them access to a path.

"Hold up," Susan said. She turned back toward Orca. "What about Rudy? Do you think we should find him and bring him too? He doesn't know that the thing will come looking for him as soon as the sun goes down."

"Susan, not trying to be a dick, but he's a dick, and he'll be more of a hindrance for us than any help. Besides, what makes you think he'll come? He didn't look very heroic as he raced by on his way to hide."

Susan took a deep breath and let it out in a long stream. She turned to Wes. "Believe it or not, Rudy has been a standup guy since you ruined our relationship. In fact, he's made a point to be a gentleman—though he might be a bit of a coward," she finished as she glanced again toward town.

"I'm sure he's been the ultimate boyfriend, but we must find Tank and Peggy right now. Once we do, we can hunt for Rudy the Saint," Wes said as he grabbed Susan by the arm.

"Speaking of that, Rudy said the bridge was gone. So, how will we get out of this place?" Bobby said.

"We'll figure it out when we're all back together. Let's go," Wes said, gently prodding Susan down the trail.

With foreboding, the trio followed the well-worn path for a few hundred yards, no one saying a word. The forest grew denser with every step, the canopy thickening above them. They walked in tense silence for what felt like hours until a foul stench hit them like a punch to the gut.

"Oh God," Susan gasped, covering her mouth. "What is that?"

Wes grimaced; his gun raised. "Something dead. Stay close."

"Don't worry, I'm right behind you," Bobby said. Wes turned and looked back. He thought Susan was there, but Bobby had moved between the two somewhere along the way. Bemused, Wes shook his head but didn't say anything.

"Do you think it might be Tank and... "Susan started, not finishing the thought.

"Let's not think that," Wes replied in a whisper.

With the stench getting stronger and stronger, they approached a bend in the trail when they heard a noise. Wes held up his hand. "Something ahead. Make sure your safeties are off on your guns, but for God's sake, let's be careful not to shoot each other."

The three inched along until they reached the bend's apex. Wes peered over a bush and saw five or six vultures feeding on a dead animal carcass. He turned back to Bobby and Susan. "Vultures eating something, but not a human."

"How the hell did they find it?" Bobby asked. "They couldn't see through this canopy. Could they?"

"They're turkey vultures," Wes explained. "They use their sense of smell to detect food—and whatever they're eating reeks."

"What now?" Bobby asked. "Should we go around?"

"No, I'll scare them away, and we'll pass through. Come on," Wes said, gripping his gun tighter. When the vultures saw the intruders, they growled, a low hissing racket of agitation.

Several began flapping their wings and hopping away. One stood its ground momentarily, daring the trio to take his prize, until an explosion of noise filled the air. It was the roar of the beast.

All the birds, including the last sentry, flew up into the vast canopy of tree branches above.

"Run," Wes ordered. The three sprinted down the trail, their feet pounding against the earth. Behind them, the creature's roar grew louder, the trees shaking with its approach.

They ran until they reached a slight incline. Wes spotted something—a backpack hanging from a low branch.

"That's Peggy's," Susan exclaimed, her voice breathless.

Wes wrenched the bag free from its purchase as he ascended the small hill but didn't stop to look inside. Once on the top of the rise, he helped Susan and Bobby up. When all three were on level ground, he looked back from where they came.

Nothing.

"I think it stopped following us," Wes said, panting.

"What now?" Bobby asked.

"From the backpack, it's clear Tank and Peggy came this way. We should keep going down the path. It might lead us to them," Wes said.

"I hope so because it's going to get dark soon. I'm not thrilled about being out here with whatever might be lurking," Susan admitted.

"I get it. Let's keep going until we find a place to camp," Wes said. "If Bobby's right, we can build a big fire. Maybe that will keep the thing away."

They walked on until the trail led them to a dead end—a wide clearing surrounded by towering granite walls, impassable vines, and thorny shrubs.

"This isn't good," Bobby muttered, glancing around.

Wes studied the area. "No, this is perfect. There's only one way in or out. Building a fire where we came up will be our best chance as it is the only way for it to get at us."

"You think fire will scare it off?" Susan asked.

"I hope so," Wes replied. "If it hates the light, maybe fire will work."

While Wes and Bobby discussed where to find firewood, Susan examined the ground near the granite wall. "Hey, guys. Check this out."

They turned as she pointed to a set of boot prints. The tracks led toward a thick patch of brush, then vanished.

Wes walked over, knelt, and pulled the vegetation aside. A cave opening revealed itself, and with it came a nauseating stench so foul it forced him to gag.

"Wow, that's God awful, way worse than whatever we passed on the trail," Susan choked out. "What could possibly smell so bad?"

"No idea, but it's a fair bet Tank and Peggy went this way, so if we are going to find them, we will have to follow. Anything in these bags to cover our noses?" Wes asked Susan.

"Maybe," Susan said as she removed her pack from her back and began going through it. She only had one bandana and nothing else they could use. She next rifled through Peggy's pack. There were a couple of rags, but nothing large enough to go around someone's head. She regarded Wes and shook her head. The two turned to Bobby.

"Are you kidding? I've got nothing," Bobby said, looking forlorn.

"Wait a minute," Susan said, returning to Peggy's backpack. After a few seconds, she pulled out a small vial of perfume. "We can dab some of this under our noses. Might help. What do you think?"

"Let's give it a try," Wes replied.

They dabbed the perfume, yet the floral scent did little to mask the putrid odor. With flashlights in hand, Wes led the way into the cave, pushing back the brush.

Inside, the darkness was suffocating. The smell grew worse with every step, a rank mixture of rot and death. The three scanned the cave with their flashlights, the beams cutting through the gloom.

At first, it seemed empty.

Then the light landed on something.

Bones.

Dozens of human bones. And—what was left of Tank Howard and Peggy Tifton.

CHAPTER 23

Discoveries

"Oh God, no!" Susan gasped, her hand flying to her mouth.

The three stood frozen, staring at the mutilated remains. Even though Tank and Peggy's heads were missing, the tattered clothes and scraps of gear left no doubt. It was them. Susan's flashlight trembled as it swept across the cave, the beam landing on a dark tunnel leading to the right.

"Look," Susan said, her voice shaking as she pointed. "There's a way out. Let's get out of here."

"What if it's waiting for us down there?" Bobby whispered as he fought back tears. He glanced at the mutilated bodies of their friends. "Look what it did to them... We could be next."

"Shhh! Quiet," Wes hissed, lifting a finger to his lips. His flashlight illuminated his tense face. "Listen."

The other two did as he bade, with Bobby doing all he could not to cry. A low growl came from outside the cave like a dog on alert if he sensed danger.

"We gotta move—now," Wes ordered as he headed toward the tunnel. They ran through the passageway for what felt like forever, the fear of the beast hot on their heels. After a few minutes, they came to a fork where three paths split off. "Which way?" Susan asked, her breath shallow, eyes darting between the dark tunnels.

"Your guess is as good as mine," Wes replied, scanning the options with his flashlight.

"South," Bobby suggested. "If we go south, we'll hit the gorge around Orca. Maybe we can find a way out from there."

"Even if we go that way, what makes you think there's a way out?" Wes asked.

"Got a better idea?" Bobby said.

"Okay. Which way is south?" Susan asked.

Bobby hesitated, then pointed to the left. "This way."

After about two hundred feet, the tunnel began to curve, and a dim light appeared. As they approached, the glow brightened, revealing a large cavern ahead.

"Uh, is that... a truck?" Susan asked, squinting at the hulking shape in the shadows.

"Yeah, it sure is. At least a part of one," Wes said, stepping closer. "Looks like an old truck cab from the '30s or '40s. How the hell did it get here?"

"Look," Susan said, shining her flashlight on the hood. "I think its dried blood."

Wes and Bobby moved in to inspect the streaks of dark red. "You're right. It is blood and a lot of it. Whoever it came from... probably didn't make it."

"I don't see any bones around here," Bobby added, his eyes searching the cave. "But I have a feeling we've already seen what's left of them."

"Let's check out the opening down there," Wes said as he pointed to the mouth of the cave. "Could be a way out."

Once at the end, Susan looked over the edge. "Hmm..."

"Yeah," Wes said, scanning the drop. "Thirty feet or more. We could climb down... but—"

"But?" Bobby asked, his anxiety spiking.

"If we get down there and there's no way out, we might not be able to climb back up," Wes said, looking left and right along the edge.

"The ocean's got to be to the right," Bobby said, trying to sound optimistic. "We could follow the shoreline and eventually find help."

"Maybe," Wes said. "What if the ravine closes off? We'll be stuck down there with nowhere to go? And even if we can get to the ocean, this part of the coast is desolate. There might not be anyone around for fifty or a hundred miles."

"I'd rather risk getting stranded on a beach than being eaten by that thing," Bobby said, his voice rising.

Wes nodded. "Fair point. Susan, what do you think?"

Susan peered down the rocky slope, hesitation clear on her face. "I don't know... If we slip while climbing, we could get seriously hurt. And even if we make it down safely, what if the ravine doesn't lead to the water?"

She glanced left, then right, frowning. "Yet, I'm with Bobby on this—I'd rather not end up as something's dinner."

"Well, we could go back and check out another tunnel. If we can't find a way out, we can always come back," Wes suggested. The three looked at each other, with no one wanting to be the one to make the choice. "Listen, if you want to stay here, I'll search the other tunnels."

"If you think I'm staying here without you, you're crazy. No offense, Bobby," Susan said.

"None taken. I wouldn't want to depend on me either," Bobby said, frowning.

"Not what I was saying. I just think we have more firepower if we stay together."

"Okay," Wes said. "Let's head back to where the tunnels split. We'll take the middle one next. If it's a dead end, we'll try the right tunnel."

"I hope we have enough time to choose another route," Bobby said, glancing around nervously. "For all we know, it could be hunting us right now."

As they passed the rusted truck cab, a faint glow appeared in the corner of the cave, catching their attention. At first, it was a dull flicker, like a dying campfire. But it quickly grew brighter, illuminating much of the cavern.

"What the hell..." Wes muttered, stopping in his tracks.

Suddenly, two figures materialized—a woman and a child, dressed in traditional Native American garb: deerskin clothes, moccasins, and long hair braided down their backs.

Then, slowly, the woman and child raised their heads to meet Wes, Susan, and Bobby's wide-eyed stares. Their eyes were hollow, dark, filled with something inhuman.

"Who... who are you?" Susan whispered, her voice barely audible.

For several moments, nothing happened, just a staring contest. And then, in eerie unison, the woman and child extended their hands and pointed at Bobby.

In voices drenched in agony and despair, they yelled, "Murderer. Killer of Wiyot. Destroyer of lives. You must die." Before Bobby could respond, the woman and child began to scream. They wailed in anguish and utter suffering. Their torment almost unbearable to hear.

To make matters worse, blood started pouring from open wounds that suddenly appeared on their faces and bodies. Their flesh tore, and then the child burst into flames, shrieking as the fire consumed her. The woman threw herself on top of the child, wailing in agony as she, too, became a flaming inferno.

Susan screamed, stumbling back. Bobby's eyes bulged, his breath churning out in sharp gasps as he shuffled backward.

Then, the flames vanished in an instant, and the cave was silent again.

"What...what the hell was that?" Bobby begged, his voice trembling. "And the smell—God, it's worse now."
"Something's coming," Wes said, gripping Susan by the arm. "Bobby, turn off your light—now!"

Bobby began fumbling with his light, trying to switch it off, but his hands and fingers didn't seem to work. He peered into the darkness, where he knew Susan and Wes stood. His face was twisted in sheer terror.

And then, a harsh scraping noise filled the area. It was a macabre sound that crept down Bobby's spine. He tried to step back, but fear held him frozen, his whole body shaking. The burning figures, the smell of decay, and the looming threat of death left him teetering on the edge of passing out. Suddenly, two glowing red eyes emerged from the blackness, barely an arm's length away.

Wes and Susan wasted no time. They opened fire, the blasts echoing through the cave. Bobby snapped out of his paralysis and stumbled back, but it was too late. The creature lunged faster than any of them expected.

Despite the barrage of bullets, the beast didn't slow. In an instant, a massive claw wrapped around Bobby's throat, lifting him off the ground. He tried to scream, but the sound was cut off as the creature's jaws slammed shut, severing his head in one swift bite.

Wes and Susan froze, horrified as they watched Bobby's lifeless body drop to the cave floor, blood pooling beneath him.

"Oh my God," Susan gasped.

The creature turned toward them, blood dripping from its mouth. It stared in their direction but oddly didn't make a move.

"We gotta go—NOW!" Wes shouted, grabbing Susan's hand. The beams from their lights bounced wildly as they bolted down the passageway.

"Here!" Wes yelled, turning into a side tunnel. "This way!"

"How do you know this goes anywhere?" Susan cried.

"I don't, but it better," Wes said, urgently.

The two ran for what seemed like forever until they came to a rise in the cave floor. The shaft sloped upwards for about twenty feet before going through a hole leading to a large wooden structure. It appeared to be what was left of an old barn.

"Thank God," Susan panted. "This is one of the barns in Orca. We can get back to base camp from here. It's only a couple hundred yards."

Wes nodded but didn't move. "Well, it's easy to see how the town of Orca disappeared. The creature probably burrowed up here and began devouring its people. If it occurred when the earthquake destroyed the bridge, there would be no place to hide. Eventually, the inhabitants would either die from starvation or be killed by the monster."

A noise from the far side of the barn made them both raise their guns.

"Is that... someone crying?" Susan asked, straining to hear.

"Who's there?" Wes called out. "We're armed! Show yourself!"

No answer, just soft whimpering.

Susan shined her light toward the sound and spotted a pair of feet sticking out from behind a crate. "Wait... I know those shoes. Rudy?"

She approached cautiously. "Rudy, is that you?"

Curled up in a ball, Rudy didn't respond. His arms were wrapped around his head, his body trembling.

"Rudy, get up!" Susan demanded, shaking his shoulder. "The monster is coming! We need to move!"

Rudy dropped his arms and lifted his head. His eyes were bloodshot and puffy from crying. "Wha...What did you say? You brought that thing here?" He stared at Susan and Wes with confusion. As the realization dawned on him, his expression turned into rage. "Get out of here. This is my place to hide."

"Rudy, we didn't bring it. And your hiding spots for shit. You'll be found and eaten before you can get five feet from here," Wes said, his voice filled with indignation.

"Eaten?" Rudy said in a gulp.

"Yeah. It killed Bobby. Bit his head clean off. And it appears Tank and Peggy came to the same end. Now get your stupid ass up, and let's..." Cravenfish didn't get to finish. A blood-curdling roar echoed from the tunnel. Wes grabbed Rudy by the scruff of the neck and jerked him up. The three ran from the building, with Rudy stumbling like a drunken sailor.

When they had made it halfway to their base camp, Wes glanced over his shoulder. A man in an Indian's wardrobe stood in the barn's doorway. Next to him was a woman and a young girl. The man inexplicably raised his hand and moved it back and forth. It was a gesture Wes couldn't comprehend.

CHAPTER 24

Sheriff Hurley's Fury

"That sassy bitch," Chief Hurley spat out, pacing his office, his heavy frame waddling with each step. His face flushed as spittle flew from his lips, and his deputy worried the chief might start foaming at the mouth. "Who the hell does she think she is? Calling me a dumbass—I'll show her who's a dumbass. I'll throw her sassy ass in jail. Damn, sassy bitch!"

"You want me to go get her?" Deputy Buttons asked, a buffoonish grin spreading across his face.

Hurley's eyes blazed. "No, you idiot."

As the chief's pants started to slip, he hitched them up in a mindless motion, still fuming. He paused, his brow furrowing in thought. "Here's what I want you to do. Round up Paul Jones, Ed Taylor, and Terry Jenkins. The four of you grab Rob Carlton's flatbed, head to their camp, and shut it down. Confiscate everything."

"Confiscate everything?" Buttons echoed, his grin fading slightly.

"That's what I said! And if they give you any trouble, arrest them all and bring them in. 'Smithsony Institution,' my ass. Let her spend a few nights in jail. Let's see how sassy she is then."

"It's the Smithsonian Institute, Chief. I get their pamphlets. Got some awesome museums and stuff. Even got the Declaration of Independence there." Buttons smiled again, clearly proud of his knowledge. Hurley glowered at him.

"Deputy, get it done," Hurley snapped, waving him off.

Buttons grabbed his hat. "On it, Chief," he said as he hurried out the door.

Deputy Buttons ran to the driver's door when Carlton arrived with his truck. Carlton glanced lazily at Buttons. "You want something, deputy?" he said, his voice dripping with derision.

"Get out, Rob. I've got to drive. This is police business," Buttons barked, trying to add authority to his demand.

Carlton didn't budge. "Might be police business, but this here's my truck," he said, the hint of a smirk tugging at his lips. "So, you wanna use it— then I'm driving. You dig?" He leaned back in his seat. "Besides, no way I'm missing you four knuckleheads going after those university eggheads. Could be a hoot watchin' you bring 'em in."

Buttons scowled and glanced at the other deputies— Jones, Taylor, and Jenkins—who sat in the patrol car, watching him with thinly veiled amusement. Their eyes gleamed, daring him to stand his ground. Buttons swallowed his pride, spat on the dirt, and slunk to the passenger side.

The deputies climbed into the back of the flatbed, a mix of nervous anticipation and excitement buzzing between them. Though they carried sidearms, none had ever drawn a weapon in a real confrontation. The prospect of it was thrilling— except for one thing. Their destination was Orca, a place cloaked in myth and dread.

Carlton turned the key, the engine roaring to life, and swung the vehicle around toward the desolate stretch known as The Lost Coast.

The farther they drove, the more the world disappeared behind them. The road was pockmarked and uneven, barely fit for a horse, let alone a truck. Thick, towering redwoods loomed over them like ancient sentinels, casting long shadows that darkened the late afternoon sky.

Though not as frigid as other regions of the country, the winter temperature could get as low as twenty degrees. Add the windy conditions caused by the Pacific Ocean breezes, and it was downright uncomfortable for several months of the year. The desolate expanse is a virgin wilderness of over sixty-seven thousand acres—yet almost all of it is unfit for human habitation.

Adding to these difficulties were the unaccounted-for missing people over the last one hundred years, not the least of which were Colonel Trevor Donaldson's settlers after World War 1. However, other disappearances were just as unexplainable. People with family histories dating back over the same time span had mysteriously vanished.

These stories and others like them have always been the obstacles to other people's attempts to live in this part of California.

"There, on the right, do you see the road?" Buttons said to Carlton.

"Yeah, I see it. Man, this is really out here. I've never come anywhere near here before."

"Why would you? The roads are piss-poor, and no one has lived out here for years—decades even. Besides, I've been told since I was a kid that the place is haunted by some kind of monster."

The word "monster" hung in the air, heavier than the truck's rattling engine.

"Monster?" Carlton said, turning his head slightly, a mock smile on his face. "That what they told you? There ain't no such thing as ghosts or goblins, you fool." But there was a flicker of uncertainty in his voice.

Buttons grimaced. "Say what you want, but plenty of folks have gone missin' 'round here, especially near Orca. Chief Hurley's had kin disappear, too. Do you think it's a coincidence he didn't come with us? He knows better than to be out here after dark. All of us should."

Carlton's smile faltered. For a moment, he considered turning his vehicle around. Buttons snapped him out of this thought when he barked, "Keep driving, Rob. We're almost there."

Carlton engaged the clutch and shifted into first. He made the turn and headed toward Orca. The truck had gone about two-thirds of a mile when they saw a car crumpled into a hundred-and-twenty-foot-tall redwood tree.

"Well, I'll be damned. I think it's the bitch's car. Pull over, and let's look. Carlton pulled in behind the crashed vehicle.

Buttons climbed out, the other men following. "Well, well. Looks like the sassy bitch drove straight into a tree. Ain't that somethin'?" Buttons smirked.

Terry Jenkins opened the driver's side door and grimaced. "Someone got hurt pretty good."

"The passenger must've smacked his head right into the windshield," Jones said, tapping the cracked glass smeared with blood and bits of skin. "Lucky he didn't break his damn neck. Wonder what made 'em crash, though. Ain't like there's traffic out here."

"Could've been a deer or something," Taylor suggested.

"Doesn't mean a hill of beans. They're not here, so they must have returned to their camp. Let's go get 'em," Buttons said as he herded the men back on the flatbed.

Carlton drove the truck up to where the archaeologists' vehicles were parked. He spun the wheel and backed toward the footbridge.

"Will you look at that? They all got flats," Jenkins said, pointing to the nearest car. "Someone knifed the tires."

Taylor crouched by one of the slashed tires, his face puzzled. "Why would anyone do this? What's the point?"

"How the hell should I know," Buttons responded. He doffed his hat and scratched vacantly at the top of his head. "Well, one thing. The grave robbers aren't getting away in these cars, that's for sure. Now grab the shotguns, and let's go."

"How do we find them? Do you know where they are?" Carlton asked Buttons.

"Nope. But I see a trail on the other side of the gorge. I bet it will lead us to their camp. Now, let's go. Oh, Rob, maybe you should remain here and watch the truck. We don't want some university egghead coming along and stealing it."

"Stay here? In these woods, alone. Are you mad? No way. I'm staying with you. Give me one of those shotguns."

"Very funny. No gun for you. If you're coming, keep behind us. You guys ready?" Buttons said to the other men. They all nodded their heads. "Ok, follow me. Let's get their asses."

Jenkins looked at Buttons and said, "Aren't we just supposed to get their gear and leave them high and dry?"

Buttons gave him a sly grin. "That was the original plan, yeah. But if we bring the woman back, Hurley will give us a bonus for sure. He hates her sassy ass. The bitch called him a dumbass to his face."

The deputies exchanged uneasy glances, but no one argued. The promise of a bonus, combined with their blind loyalty to Chief Hurley, sealed their fate.

The men continued down the narrow trail, the forest thickening around them. The trees pressed closer, the air growing colder with every step. Shadows stretched long and twisted, playing tricks on their minds.

After a while, Carlton couldn't take it anymore. "What if we don't find 'em before dark?" he muttered, his voice shaky.

Buttons at first didn't answer. The wind rustled the leaves, and the eerie quiet of the woods seemed to swallow the question whole.

"We'll find 'em," Buttons vowed, though the conviction in his tone was wearing thin. He could feel the weight of the forest bearing down on them, a sensation something—or someone—was watching.

They trudged on, the sense of dread growing with each passing minute.

Suddenly, Jenkins froze, his eyes wide with fear. "Did... did you hear that?"

A long, low growl echoed from somewhere deep within the forest, sending a chill down their spines.

Carlton's breath hitched. "Tell me that wasn't what I think it was."

Buttons clenched his jaw, gripping his shotgun tighter. "Keep going," he ordered, his demand betraying the first hint of dread. "We're almost there."

They pushed forward, but each step felt heavier and more labored. Behind them, the sound of something large moving through the trees—sniffing and stalking—grew louder.

Carlton's voice trembled as he whispered, "Maybe... maybe we should turn back."

Yet there was no turning back. They were already in too deep.

CHAPTER 25

Flight from the Beast

"Susan, are there any flares in the camp?" Wes asked.

"I think so," she replied, her brow furrowed in confusion. "Why?"

"With the bridge down, we'll need another way off this place, which might take some time. I'm hoping that the flares will keep it at bay until we can get out of here."

Rudy, still shaking in the corner, whimpered, "Are you insane? We can't fight this... thing." His voice cracked.

Wes turned to Rudy, his eyes narrowing into an icy glare. "Stevens, get a grip," he said, his tone edged with annoyance. "You're whimpering like a damn infant. Secondly, I'm not talking about fighting it. I'm talking about holding it off long enough to find a way out."

For a brief second, Wes wanted to slap him—partly to jolt him out of his terror, but mostly because it was tempting, and he would enjoy it.

Shaking his head, Wes refocused on Susan. "There was a Jeep among the cars. We'll need the keys. It might be easier to drive, even with a flat."

"That's Tank's Jeep," she said, her voice catching. "I just hope he didn't have the keys on him..." She trailed off, the gruesome image of Tank's decapitated body flashing in her mind. A wave of nausea hit her. Closing her eyes, she inhaled deeply, willing herself to stay composed. "I'll check his things for the keys. If we have flares, they should be in one of the crates over there." She pointed to a stack near the supply tent.

By the time Wes finished gathering the needed supplies, dusk was creeping in, casting long, menacing shadows across the camp. He had found a dozen flares, two boxes of matches, a hatchet, and a small can of kerosene. He also unearthed two more cartons of shells for the shotguns. When he stepped out of the tent, Susan was waiting, the Jeep keys dangling from her fingers.

"I located the keys—and this." She held up a large hunting knife in its sheath.

"Good," Wes said, nodding approvingly. "Let's head to where the bridge was and start searching for a way across. The ravine might narrow further north. We already know it doesn't narrow to the south—we saw that in the caves. Yet I have to believe there must be a way to cross. Once we find it, we'll head for the Jeep, drive to the sheriff's office, and tell him what's happening."

Susan scoffed. "The sheriff's office? Yeah, excellent idea. I can't wait to tell him there really is a monster here. He'll lock us up for sure That jackass won't do anything. Besides, I think he knows something about this and isn't telling us…"

Wes's jaw tightened, but he kept his voice level. "Maybe. Though I'm hoping when he hears there've been murders, and we threaten to go to the Associated Press about his lack of action, he'll have no choice but to take it seriously."

"Or..." she shot back, her tone dripping with sarcasm, "he'll arrest us for causing a panic and throw away the key."

****

"Buttons, do you have any clue where we are?" Jenkins's words came out strained, his eyes darting between the looming trees as they trudged along the trail. "Feels like we've been walking forever and getting nowhere."

Deputy Buttons, keeping his gaze fixed on the thinning path ahead, wiped the sweat from his brow. "Can't be much further. Christ, we'll hit the damn ocean if we keep going like this."

Jenkins shifted uneasily. "I'm thinking we should've taken the left trail back at that Y in the trail. The right one doesn't feel like it's leading anywhere. I bet the left would've led us straight to the town—what's left of it."

Buttons grunted, his patience waning, "Yeah, maybe so. Wait—hold on a second." He squinted as they rounded a bend. "There's a clearing up ahead. Told you I'd find the damn place."

The other men, Jones and Taylor, edged closer to see what Buttons had spotted.

"Hey, who's that?" Jones pointed toward a figure sprinting across the open field, fast as a deer fleeing a predator. "Man, he's booking it."

"Why would he be running like that? Is something chasing him?" Jenkins asked.

"Not that I can see," Buttons said, shading his eyes. "Wait—there's more. I see a group standing by those tents. Three of 'em...and one of 'em looks like that sassy bitch Hurley's so riled up about. The guy's running right for them…and now he's running right past them. What the heck?" Buttons murmured.

"He's heading for the town. Should we go take care of business while that fella's gone? One less person to deal with," Jones said.

Buttons thought about this and said, "Let's see what the people at the camp do first. Then we'll decide if we…"

But before anyone could respond, a thunderous roar shattered the air, sending a jolt of terror through the group. The ground beneath them shook, the sheer force of the sound overwhelming. Deputy Buttons dropped to the dirt, covering his ears, memories of artillery blasts from the war in Germany flashing through his mind. The other deputies flinched, eyes wide, hands trembling.

"Oh, sweet Jesus, what was that?" Jenkins gasped, voice cracking as he instinctively backed up.

"I don't know, but I'm going home and never leaving my house again," Ed Taylor shouted. Without waiting for orders, he spun on his heels and bolted back the way they came, panic driving him like an animal fleeing a fire.

Jenkins and Jones exchanged one last horrified glance before following Taylor, their feet pounding the dirt in blind desperation.

They ran for what felt like an eternity, the adrenaline hammering in their veins. After thirty minutes, their gasps for breath were as loud as their footfalls, and the forest began to thin again. As they approached the clearing where Carlton's truck was parked, Jenkins slowed, confusion etching into his face.

"Where's the bridge?" Taylor's voice was a strangled cry. "It's gone! The goddamn bridge is gone!"

"What are you talking about? How does a bridge just disappear? We must be at the wrong place," Jenkins yelled as he hurried up behind Taylor.

Taylor jabbed a finger toward the vehicles. "There's the grave robbers' cars and Carlton's truck. We're in the right place, alright. But where the hell's the crossing?"

The men moved to where the wooden span used to be. Taylor looked over the ravine's edge. "Well, I found the bridge."

"You've got to be kidding me. Now, what are we going to do? How we going to get out of here?" Jones pleaded.

As they looked at the wrecked structure at the bottom of the ravine, a low, rumbling growl emanated from the forest behind them. The men turned and froze. They watched as a giant creature came trudging out. It was the most hideous, foul, and horrifying vision any of them had ever seen. Even the foulest nightmare imagined couldn't come close to what they witnessed.

The thing was easily fifteen feet tall and half as wide, covered in metal-looking scales and squirming eel-like arms emerging from the top of its head. As he approached, the beast's jaw hinged opened, revealing rows of jagged, razor-sharp teeth, and the stench of its breath hit them like a physical blow. The smell was so overpowering it made Jenkins gag, his stomach turning violently.

For a moment, none of the men moved. They were rooted to the spot, paralyzed by the sheer horror of what stood before them. The creature stalked closer; its movements eerily smooth for something of its size. When it was within ten feet, its massive maw widened further, exposing a pit of darkness lined with those deadly teeth.

Jones and Taylor broke first, instincts overriding terror. Without a word, they scattered in opposite directions, leaving Jenkins standing alone, trembling uncontrollably.

Jenkins couldn't move. He was locked in place, shock freezing his muscles. The beast loomed closer, filling his vision. Its eyes bored into him, and the rancid smell intensified, making him vomit on the spot. He could feel warmth running down his leg—his bladder releasing involuntarily. His breaths came in ragged, choking gasps as he realized there was no escape.

"No, no, no," Jenkins whimpered, shrinking down in fear. "Please... please, don't hurt me."

The creature stopped inches from him, towering over the deputy. It tilted its massive head, studying him with an unnerving curiosity. Then, in a voice more demonic than human, the beast rumbled, "You are not a killer of my people."

Jenkins blinked, barely able to comprehend the words. His lips trembled. "No, no, I've killed no one. I don't even know who your people are!"

The monster exhaled loudly, a sound like a deflating bellows. The large red orbs in its face narrowed.

"Hmmm…" the thing moaned. "No matter. You are white man. All white men are evil," Before Jenkins could respond, it lunged with blinding speed. One clawed arm shot out, seizing his right arm in a crushing grip. With one swift motion, it ripped the arm clean from his body, sending a spray of blood into the air. Jenkins's scream was inhuman, piercing the stillness of the forest like an alarm.

****

"Buttons," Rob Carlton yelled. "Get your ass up, or I'm leaving you here. "Come on!" Carlton grabbed the deputy under the armpits and lifted the man to his feet. He turned him around to where they were face to face.

Buttons' eyes were wide, tears streaming down his face. "What... what could make a sound like that? For a minute there, I thought I was back in the trenches. It shook me to my soul..." he stammered.

"I don't know, and I don't want to know. Right now, I only care about getting out of here. And if you don't snap out of it, I'm leaving you behind, and you can find out what made the noise on your own."

"Okay. Okay, don't go without me. Please. I'm coming," Buttons sobbed.

Carlton turned and raced off, with Buttons doing his best to stay close. The trail was a long, winding, tree-covered pathway, and though it was still afternoon, the canopy darkened the entire area as if the sun was setting. The shadows moved like undulating seaweed, causing both men to flinch and jump as they thought something was about to rush from the trees to get them.

"Shouldn't be much further," Carlton called over his shoulder.

"Yeah, I remember this spot. The bridge can't be more than a couple of hundred feet. At that moment, a scream rang out. It was not the same roar from whatever made the previous noise but a man's shriek. And it was one of terrifying intensity and pain. "My God, was that Jenkins? What the hell is happening."

The two rounded a corner and skidded to a halt.

A huge, unholy being was eviscerating Terry Jenkins. His right arm was gone, and then, as if pulling a leaf from a tree, his right arm was off. Jenkins's eyes were bulging and looked like they might pop clean out of his head. He kept screaming and trying to wriggle free, but the beast ignored his efforts.

When Carlton and Buttons thought they might faint dead away from the scene unfolding before them, the beast turned and looked their way. Its eyes were glowing red orbs the size of large saucers. Its mouth, easily as big as a car tire, was chewing something, and then it swallowed. As if the thing was giving them a sign of what to expect, it opened its jaws wide and cleaved Jenkins' head off in one bite.

"Okay, time to go," Carlton blurted. "Run as fast as you can back the way we came. I'll be right behind you." And both did run. They ran like their lives depended on it. Twice, Buttons tripped and fell, and Carlton had to drag him back to his feet each time. When it happened a third time, Carlton didn't stop.

He leaped over Buttons' fallen body and kept running, his breath ragged, panic overriding any sense of loyalty.

"Wait. Rob, come back. I think I twisted my ankle."

"You're on your own, buddy," Carlton shouted without looking back. "I'm not stopping!"

"Please, Rob, don't leave me," Buttons cried. He finally got to his feet and tried to put weight on his injured right ankle. He shifted back and forth on each foot, realizing it didn't hurt too badly. He started after Carlton but at a slower pace. He looked back every few minutes, preying that the monster wasn't after him.

The forest was silent for now.

When Paul Jones escaped the creature, he veered left, sprinting toward the main trail in a blind panic. His breath came in ragged gasps as his feet pounded against the leaf-covered ground.

After a while, he risked a glance over his shoulder, half expecting the monstrous thing to be right behind him. But the woods were eerily quiet, except for the hammering of his heartbeat in his ears. Relief flooded him, and he slowed to a stop, turning to where the confrontation with Jenkins had taken place.

"Come on, Terry... run. Run, buddy, please. Get out of there," Jones muttered, his eyes straining through the dimming light.

When the creature tore Jenkins's arm off with a sickening rip, Jones' stomach lurched. He watched in horror as the beast bent down and, with one terrifying bite, decapitated his friend.

Jones shrieked, panic overriding any semblance of rational thought. He spun on his heel and bolted into the darkening forest, his screams echoing through the trees as he fled.

On the other hand, Ed Taylor hadn't dared to look back after he'd gotten away. His mind had snapped into survival mode, and he'd darted right, circling behind the creature and disappearing into the woods where it had first emerged. He didn't care where he was going—he just needed to put as much distance as possible between him and that... thing.

The path was rough, overgrown with vines and thick underbrush. The beast had forged its own way, tearing through the dense foliage like a bulldozer, leaving chaos in its wake.

Taylor stumbled and clawed his way forward, unknowing and uncaring, his legs burning with exertion. After an undeterminable time, he came to a more defined trail. Turning right, he followed it for a few more minutes until the clearing with the archaeologists' camp and the ruined town of Orca came into view.

"Help! Please, help me!" Taylor screamed; his voice hoarse. But there was no response. The camp lay still.

Panting, he staggered toward the campsite, frantically searching everywhere for any sign of life. When he yanked back the flap of Julia's tent, the stench hit him like a punch to the gut. The smell of rot and decay was overpowering, sending him reeling backward. His stomach twisted, and he doubled over.

"What in God's name have these people unleashed?" Taylor gasped between heaves. "This has to be Satan himself. I've got to get out of here."

He wiped his mouth, eyes scanning the empty tents and the shadowy outline of Orca in the distance. Running there crossed his mind, but the town clung to a cliff plunging into the ocean—no escape that way. His gaze shifted to a narrow gap in the forest on his right.

He took a hesitant step toward it, then stopped, his instincts screaming. "Are you crazy, Taylor?" he muttered. "You can't go in there. Not alone."

Spinning around, he scanned the tree line to the north— just then, he saw Rob Carlton burst out of the woods. Carlton was running like a man possessed, his face twisted with fear.

"Rob!" Taylor shouted, frantically waving his arms to get Carlton's attention. At first, Carlton didn't seem to notice. Taylor jumped up and down, yelling until his voice cut through, and Carlton finally looked his way. Just then, Deputy Buttons staggered out of the trees behind Carlton, pale and unsteady.

Without hesitating, Taylor bolted toward them, his arms flailing as he closed the gap. By the time he was twenty yards away, he was babbling a jumble of words, struggling to explain what had happened to Jenkins.

"Hold on, Ed!" Carlton said, raising a hand to calm him. "Take a breath before you pass out. We saw it, too. We watched the whole thing happen."

Taylor's chest heaved as he gulped for air. "It was... it was horrible!"

Carlton nodded grimly. "Yeah, it was. And now the bridge is gone. We're trapped with a real goddamn monster on the loose."

"What are we going to do?" Taylor's voice cracked with desperation. "How do we get out of here?"

Carlton glanced at the darkening sky. "I don't know, but it will be night soon, and I don't want to be anywhere near here when that happens."

"What about the town?" Buttons interjected; his tone shaky. "We could hide there. The chief will send someone to find us when we don't come back. Orca might be the safest place until help arrives."

Carlton shook his head. "I think that's a terrible idea. For all we know, the monster lives in one of those buildings. No, we need to head toward the ocean and go north. Maybe the ravine doesn't stretch all the way around."

"That's a good plan. A great plan!" Taylor's panic ratcheted up another notch. "Let's go! Now!" He didn't wait for a response and bolted toward the ocean, his feet barely touching the ground.

Carlton watched him for a moment. He turned to Buttons. "Are you coming or staying, Deputy?"

Buttons hesitated, glancing back at the camp. "What about the grave robbers? We were supposed to shut them down."

Carlton's face hardened. "Buttons, you are something. Believe me, they're shut down. The monster made sure of that." Without another word, Carlton took off after Taylor, leaving Buttons no choice but to follow.

CHAPTER 26

FLEE!

"Can you think of anything else we need from the camp?" Wes asked as he jogged alongside Susan and Rudy. "We've got the flares, some water, our flashlights, and the guns."

"Not me," Rudy panted. "And even if I did, I'm not sticking around to gather it up."

"Yeah. I'm with him on this one. Let's get out of here," Susan said.

Stephenson looked at her with a confused expression. What did she mean by that—I'm with him on this one. He was about to question his girlfriend when he saw some men on the far side of the clearing running away from where they stood.

"Look over there," Rudy said, pointing. "Three guys running toward the ocean. Who do you think they are?"

Susan squinted into the distance, shading her eyes against the setting sun. "Is that...? Could it be...?" She paused. "Isn't that the deputy from the police station in the back? The one with the stupid ass grin? The idiot Hurley sent his men to harass us. Bet they wish they'd stayed home."

"Me too," Rudy muttered under his breath.

Wes ignored the back-and-forth, still focused on the fleeing figures. "It could be the deputy. Maybe they know something we don't about getting out of here."

"Should we go after them?" Susan asked.

Wes shook his head. "I don't think so. We need to stick to the plan—get to the ravine and follow it north. We might end up in the same place they're heading, but if the only crossing is along the ravine, I don't want to risk backtracking and running into our gruesome friend."

"Fine, we're right behind you," Susan agreed.

Wes reached into his jacket and pulled out a pistol, handing it to Rudy. "Here, take this."

Rudy eyed the gun with a mixture of skepticism and fear. "What good is this gonna do against that big-ass thing he scoffed."

Wes shot him a cold stare. "Give it back, then." Rudy

stuck the pistol in his belt. "Nope, I'll keep it."

"Though you might," Wes mocked.

They set off toward the ravine, Wes leading at a steady pace. When they reached the spot where the footbridge once stood only the gaping abyss remained. A decapitated, armless body lay near where the bridge had collapsed.

"My God," Susan whispered, recoiling in horror. "Just like Tank and Peggy... I wonder who this poor guy was."

Rudy, pale and trembling, could only stare. He couldn't force the words from his throat, the sight rendering him mute.

Wes crouched near the corpse. "Looks like one of the deputies. Hard to tell with all the blood, but I'm sure it's a police uniform." He stood abruptly. "We can't stop. Let's keep moving."

They followed a narrow trail running parallel to the ravine's edge. Sometimes, it clung close to the chasm; other times, it veered inland, swallowed by thick, overgrown brush.

The sky had darkened quickly, forcing them to rely on their flashlights. After thirty minutes without finding a way across, Rudy gasped for breath and asked, "Can we rest for a second or two?"

Before anyone could answer, a deafening roar echoed through the night, the sound so primal it shook the ground beneath their feet.

"NOPE!" Rudy shrieked, already moving again. "No need to rest!"

"That sound... it's terrifying," Susan said, her voice barely above a whisper. "Every time I hear it; my heart skips a beat."

"Stay with me," Wes urged, picking up the pace. The trail grew rougher, dense with underbrush and low-hanging branches. "Hold on. Something's up ahead on the ground."

"Oh, great," Rudy groaned. "What now? A rattlesnake?"

Wes moved closer, shining his flashlight on the object. "It's not a snake," he said, bending down to pick it up. "It's a rifle."

He held the weapon up for Susan and Rudy to see. The name K. Tucker was etched into the stock.

"K. Tucker?" Wes murmured. "Why would he leave his rifle here?"

Susan crossed her arms. "Maybe K stands for Karen or Kathy. Why assume it's a guy?"

Wes shot her a look. "Really? You want to argue now? Fine—whatever the K stands for, why did they abandon their rifle? It's a little weather-beaten, but other than that, it looks fine."

Rudy's voice dropped to a whisper. "Because the monster ate them. It didn't care about the gun... just the person's head."

Wes paused, his eyes narrowing. "Susan... wasn't one of the people we talked about earlier named Tucker? A boy, I think. Went missing with his dog while hunting. This could be his gun."

Susan nodded, her face pale. "Yeah, I think you're right."

Wes turned his flashlight toward the ravine. A fallen redwood spanned the chasm about twenty feet away, forming a natural bridge.

"Thank God," Rudy exhaled. "Let's go."

Susan didn't waste a second. "We need to get to Tank's Jeep."

"Right behind you, babe," Rudy said, attempting a grin.

Susan stopped mid-step, her eyes flashing. "Rudy, you can stop calling me babe. After the way you left me behind— twice—I'm done. And you'd better keep up if you don't want me to leave you behind." She pushed past him, climbing onto the redwood.

Before she started to cross, a rustling noise from the woods made her freeze.

"Quick, get behind me. And turn your lights off," Wes whispered. The other two did as he asked, though Rudy let out a moan of dread as he moved around Susan.

Suddenly, voices cut through the night.

"Shit! What happened to the trail?" someone groaned. "I can't get through these damn thorny vines."

"Shut up, Buttons!" a second voice snapped. "Didn't you hear that thing? Do you want to be its next meal?"

Wes stepped forward; flashlight raised. "Who's there?"

"Jones, is that you? It's me, Carlton. Buttons and Taylor are with me, too. You alright?" Rob Carlton replied.

"No, it's not Jones. It's Wes Cravenfish. There are three of us. We found a way to get across the ravine."

"Oh, sweet Jesus. The chasm goes all the way to the ocean. There's nowhere north of here to cross," Carlton said.

Buttons moved forward and, jutting out his chest, said, "You're under arrest! Whatever you unleashed out here—it killed one of my men, and you're responsible. Hands up!"

Carlton rolled his eyes. "You really are an idiot, after all. No one's under arrest, not now, anyway. We need to get the hell out of here before we're all dead. Save the accusations for later."

"Well, maybe you're right. Okay, but no funny business," Buttons drawled.

Wes shook his head in disbelief. "Susan, you go first. Rudy, you're next." He handed his flashlight to Carlton. "I'll follow after you."

Susan climbed onto the tree and began crossing. Rudy followed, but instead of walking, he dropped to his hands and knees, crawling slowly.

Halfway across, Rudy's flashlight slipped from his grip and tumbled into the abyss.

"Rudy, you idiot!" Wes hissed. "Get up and keep moving!"

"I can't!" Rudy whimpered, his voice breaking. "I'll fall!"

Wes's temper flared. "If you don't get moving, I'll shove you into the ravine myself."

But Rudy remained frozen, his body trembling with fear. Susan, having reached the other side, turned her flashlight on him. "What the hell? Rudy, get up and move!"

"I can't. I'm stuck. My body won't move."

A sound like a Sherman tank crashing through the foliage shattered the tense silence. When the creature roared, Rudy sprang to his feet, eyes wide with panic, and bolted across the tree with Wes close behind.

Carlton and Taylor climbed onto the redwood and hurried toward the other side. Buttons was pulling himself up when another roar rang out. The terrifying noise startled him, causing him to lose his grip and fall. He scrambled to his feet, clambering back onto the tree just as the creature burst through the underbrush.

"Wait for me!" Buttons cried, his voice a high-pitched wail of terror. "I can't see! Someone shine a light!"

Susan turned her flashlight toward him—and what she saw made her blood run cold. "Oh God, it's right behind you!" she screamed.

Buttons turned to see how close his pursuer was. The thing was only a few feet away. He tried to flee—but it was too late. The beast reached out and grabbed the man's arm. The deputy screeched in terror and tried to jerk free. He pulled, tugged, and hit the monster with his other fist and kicked at it with his feet. But escape was impossible, and in seconds, his head was gone, and his body was falling into the chasm, a lifeless flip-flopping corpse.

"He's gone!" Wes yelled. "We've gotta move!"

They all ran, five terrified humans fleeing from a relentless predator. Behind them, the beast roared, lumbering after them with terrifying speed.

"There!" Carlton shouted. "I see the truck!"

Once at the truck, Susan handed Wes her flashlight and climbed into the passenger seat while the others clambered onto the back. Carlton floored the gas pedal just as the creature burst from the trees.

Wes aimed the flashlight out the back window, catching a glimpse of the monster. It had dropped to all fours, chasing them with unnatural agility. His beam also caught something else—a figure on the other side of the ravine, waving for all their worth.

"There's someone over there!" Wes called out. "Is he one of your men?"

Taylor's eyes widened. "Oh God, it's Paul. I forgot about him."

CHAPTER 27

Beneath the Surface

The phone rang insistently at the Capetown police station. It was six in the evening, and Polly Bedford, the daytime attendant, had left for the day. Her replacement, Ida Lynn Dillon, hadn't yet made it to the desk. The ringing persisted for several minutes until Chief Hurley, his patience thin, stormed out of his office and toward the reception area.

"This better be good," Hurley barked into the receiver, not bothering to mask his irritation.

"Well, hello to you too, Chief," came the familiar voice of his wife, Gloria, on the other end of the line.

Hurley's tone softened. "Oh, sorry, dear. What can I do for you?"

"I'm heading to Liza's to drop off some chicken soup. Little Mary's sick—croup or something—so I thought I'd help. I've also packed you a plate: slices of ham, pole beans, and a big piece of the chocolate cake you love. Figured you'd like some dinner since you're working late tonight."

"Oh, you sure know how to win a man's love, my dear. You are one of a kind. I await your generous offering with a glad heart—and stomach," Gloria's husband said with dripping heartfelt appreciation.

"And you sure know how to sweet-talk, Chief. I'll see you in about an hour," Gloria said, her voice warm, before hanging up.

"Dang it," Hurley said as he stared out the front door. He took a moment to think what he should do, shook his head, and walked back toward his office. On the way, the widow, Ida Lynn Dillon, was heading his way. As they were about to pass each other, Hurley started to mention the call with his wife, but Ida Lynn stifled the comment when she reached out and placed her hand on his penis and squeezed.

"Uh—" Hurley's eyes darted around though he knew no one else was in the station. Polly had left, and his deputies were off dealing with the situation in Orca. His mind raced, but the physical sensation overrode his thoughts—and judgment.

"Well, don't you have a way with words," Ida Lynn said with a sultry smile, continuing to rub his now-hardening length through his pants. Hurley blushed, a wave of guilt mingling with desire. His wife had said something similar on the phone moments earlier.

"You want to fool around before I get to work?" Ida Lynn whispered, her fingers tracing the outline of him through his slacks. "I could, you know... if you want."

Hurley swallowed hard, his eyes fluttering as her touch grew more insistent. "I've been thinkin' about it all afternoon," he admitted in a low voice. "Told Gloria I'd be workin' late so we could, uh... have a little fun. But she called a few minutes ago and said she's bringin' me dinner, so... she's on her way." Ida Lynn's grip tightened slightly more than expected.

"Now honey, don't do this. You know I'm on your side. But I've got kids at home, so I need to be careful."

"Yeah, I get it," Ida Lynn replied with a frown. She gave him one last pat, her lips curling into a playful smile before slipping past him. Hurley reached down, trying to adjust himself. His member was tangled in his underpants, but his large stomach made it nearly impossible.

The front door buzzer sounded.

"Well, hello there, Mrs. Hurley. What a surprise," Ida Lynn said, her voice polite and professional.

"Hello, Ida Lynn. I called the Chief and told him I'd drop supper. He said he'd be working a little late tonight…"

Yeah, working a little late on me, Ida Lynn thought.

"…and I knew he'd get hungry. So, here I am. Is he around?"

"Oh, yes, Mrs. Hurley. I ran into him in the hall a moment ago. We had a lovely conversation about our day so far. He's such a thoughtful boss. Always going out of his way to do kind things for me." Ida Lynn smiled with false innocence. "But I think he stepped into the restroom. I can take the food to his office if you'd like?"

"No thank you," Gloria said, her tone sharp enough to convey that she preferred to see her husband herself. "I'll take it to him. I'm sure you've got work to do."

Hearing the two women talking drained the lust from the man's penis like someone pulling the plug in a sink. He waddled back to his office and sat behind his desk, brooding over the tangled web his life had become.

Gloria wasn't just his wife. She had been his childhood sweetheart. The two played kids' games together when they were young, only for those games to grow more complicated and adult in high school.

As a teenager, Hurley reigned as the ultimate jock. He was the captain of his high school football and baseball teams for all three years—a feat no other student had accomplished. In addition to excelling in those sports, he was a key member of the district-winning wrestling team until a back injury during a match sidelined him for two weeks.

Fearing for his star quarterback, the football coach convinced Hurley's parents to forbid him from participating in wrestling for the rest of his high school days.

Gloria Elizabeth Tillson was taller than most girls and many boys throughout her school days. In fact, she was almost as tall as Hurley. Though rail-thin through ninth grade, by the time she was a high school junior, she had developed a real woman's shape, which was unusual for those times.

Daniel and Gloria's relationship had been purely platonic until Hurley saw her in her cheerleader's uniform as a sophomore. The sight altered everything. Gloria Tilson was no longer just a female friend or schoolmate; she became someone he and every other boy desired.

Tillson was a natural blond with hazel eyes, a straight nose, narrow nostrils, and high cheekbones. Her skin was Dove Bar white and without a blemish. Toss in her great hips, tiny waist, and big, beautiful breasts, and Gloria went from next-door tomboy to absolute knockout woman.

Yes, she was something back then, and to Hurley's advantage, Gloria was smitten with him. She fawned over him every time they were together and never stopped him from the occasional but often awkward fondling when they made out. And when they went to the lake in his dad's thirty-six Chevy Coupe, Gloria let him get to third base without any resistance. She would have allowed him to go all the way; it's what she wanted. But the eager young boy hadn't lasted long enough to get there.

Gloria's parents never liked Hurley and wanted him out of their daughter's life before something happened. Yes, they'd put up with their daughter's puppy love, but it was time to start applying for college, and she needed to forget Hurley. The boy was going nowhere, and they knew it. But more to the point, they knew where the relationship was headed, and they couldn't let anything untold happen.

During a heated argument, Gloria declared she would attend school wherever Daniel went. Mr. and Mrs. Tilson, determined to prevent this, insisted she apply to universities in the east—far from Daniel. Before long, she was accepted to Vassar, and the discussion ended.

Her parents ultimatum decimated Gloria. But once Vassar was imminent, she knew Daniel had to be told. She decided to wait until after their senior graduation party to tell Daniel about having to attend college in New York. She didn't want to ruin the party for him, though the news ruined it for her.

After getting their diplomas, the football jocks and their girlfriends had a party at one of the parent's houses by the lake. Several of the boys had stolen booze, Gordon's Gin, and Walnut Hill Rye, and many got drunk.

Hurley had offered a drink to Gloria early in the evening, hoping to get her 'in the mood' because this time, he'd get to home plate with her—for sure. After all, it was graduation night. But she'd refused it. And, in fact, had stayed away from him most of the night. This caused him to drink to excess.

As the evening wore on, Gloria complained to one of the other girls about the boys drinking too much. During the conversation, she let it slip that she was happy she was going to Vassar and leaving all the immature boys of Capetown behind. A girl who overheard the comment told her boyfriend. He found Hurley and told him.

Hurley was beyond despondent and confronted Gloria in one of the bedrooms. When she confirmed the news, he began crying and was inconsolable. Tillson couldn't bear it and embraced her boyfriend for forgiveness. She kissed him, saying she was sorry. This kiss led to another and another.

Soon after, the two were making out with intense lust, pawing at one another with abandon. The next thing Gloria knew, they were naked, and Daniel Hurley was inside of her. It was what she'd always wanted. But something wasn't right, and she became scared.

Gloria begged Hurley to stop and get off. But it was too late.

Before leaving for Vassar that summer, Gloria discovered she was pregnant. She had no choice but to inform her parents.

They reached out to the Hurleys, and the four parents sat the couple down, declaring they had to marry. Daniel and Gloria, furious and blaming each other, wanted nothing to do with the idea.

Despite their resistance, they married over the summer before Gloria began showing. The couple moved in with her parents, though they refused to share a bedroom. Seven months later, Roger Benjamin Hurley was born.

Daniel was drafted in 1942 and served in the motor pool as well as an MP in Patton's 2nd Armored Division in Europe. After returning to the United States in mid-1945, he went to work as a deputy for his father, Willard Hurley.

By then, he and Gloria had moved out of her parent's home into a small two-bedroom house in town. Though still not enamored with one another's company, they survived. Gloria loved their son, and their son loved his daddy. So, they endured. When the senior Hurley died of liver cancer ten years later, his son became sheriff.

This new position suited Gloria and soothed their relationship—for a while. But Daniel got fat and power-hungry—both traits his wife loathed. Gloria kept up appearances in public, but their private lives once again were in shambles—and sex, forget about it.

That's when Ida Lynn Dillon entered the picture.

Ida Lynn's family left Chicago when she was thirteen. Her father claimed the city had become too rough to raise kids and decided to relocate the family to Ferndale, a sleepy town where they had distant relatives. Ida Lynn hated Ferndale from the onset.

Chicago had been exciting, vibrant, full of possibilities. Ferndale, by contrast, felt suffocating—dull, backward, and out of sync with the rest of the world. The town was stuck in time, with nothing but small-town gossip and quiet desperation to offer.

By the time she hit tenth grade, Ida Lynn was practically invisible. Her figure was boyish—more string bean than woman. She had no curves to speak of. Her auburn hair hung limp and greasy, and her dark green eyes seemed set too far back in her round, unremarkable face. She wasn't unattractive, but nothing about her stood out enough to draw attention. She drifted through high school like a shadow, overlooked by the boys and disregarded by the girls.

When she returned for her senior year, everything had changed.

Somehow, over the course of one summer, Ida Lynn transformed. Her body filled out in all the right places, and she went from plain to undeniably pretty—maybe not stunning, but certainly attractive. Her stringy hair was cut into a sleek bob, framing her slimmer face and highlighting the freckles scattered across her nose and cheeks.

Ida Lynn's dull green eyes now glowed with a vivid emerald intensity, captivating anyone who met her gaze. Her figure had also changed, with a full, rounded chest, a cinched waist, and hips that curved into a shapely bottom, drawing the attention of boys and men alike as she passed.

The change was nothing short of magical, and Ida Lynn reveled in the newfound attention. By the time she reached her early twenties, she had an apartment and a job waiting tables at McGuire's Diner in downtown Ferndale. But waiting tables wasn't her endgame. Her plan was simple: save enough money to leave town or, better yet, meet someone who would take her far away from the life she despised.

When her father died of a heart attack at fifty-one, Ida Lynn had hoped for an inheritance. She imagined the money would finally give her the freedom she craved. But instead, she learned her father had been drowning in debt.

Far from receiving any windfall, Ida Lynn had to dig into her savings to help her mother keep their family home. It was a cruel blow but not an unfamiliar one. Life had always seemed to keep her trapped.

Then, when she was twenty-five, good fortune and promise came her way.

It was during the Ferndale County Fair, and Ida Lynn was working the ticket booth. During her shift, she met Peter Blanton, a handsome truck driver and deliveryman. Ida Lynn recognized his type at once. She could tell by how he looked at her that his intentions were far from honorable, but she saw an opportunity.

Ida Lynn would let him think he was in control and believe he was winning her over with his looks and smooth talk. But she'd be the one setting the trap. She knew how men like Peter operated and how to use those behaviors to her advantage.

After the fair, Blanton invited her back to his motel room. Ida Lynn played hard to get at first, feigning offense at his boldness. She pushed him away when he tried to kiss her, teasing him only enough to make him want her more.

When he pulled out a bottle of Jim Beam and asked if she'd like a drink, she hesitated—for show—and then agreed. They went back to his room, and Ida Lynn made sure it was a night Peter Blanton wouldn't forget.

As she dressed the next morning, taking her time and letting him watch, she knew she had him hooked. She'd played the part to perfection. Before leaving, she delivered her well rehearsed lines.

"Peter, I had a delightful time. You were... well, let's say you were more experienced than I expected. I felt things last night I didn't know I could feel." She bit her lower lip as she spoke, adding just the right amount of sensuality to her words. "But there's something you should know..."

Blanton's eyes widened, his breath quickening.

"There's a boy in town. Ronny Smith. He works at his father's bank. He's asked my mother for my hand." She sighed, playing the part of the conflicted, small-town girl. "It's fast, I know. But in Ferndale, there aren't many choices. We've only gone on a few dates, and I've never done what you and I did last night with him."

Blanton ate it up and swore he'd be back the following week. "Don't let some country bumpkin tie you down, Ida," he said. "You wait for me."

She smiled with sweet innocence, blew him a kiss, and walked out of the room. As soon as the door closed behind her, she allowed herself a triumphant laugh. *Got him hook, line, and sinker*, she mused.

But Blanton never came back. The following week, and the week after, she waited. No one from his company returned until three weeks later, and it wasn't Peter. The new driver informed his customers that Blanton and one of their trucks had disappeared. No one had seen or heard from him since his last delivery.

For Ida Lynn, it was devastating. Her well-thought-out plan to escape Ferndale had collapsed. Worse still, she soon discovered she was pregnant. The ensuing shame she faced was unbearable. The town's gossip mill churned with cruel whispers, and soon no one would speak to her. To them, she was a harlot, a girl who couldn't keep her legs closed.

When her son, Billy, was born, Ida Lynn packed up her meager belongings and left Ferndale for good, moving south to Capetown hoping to start fresh.

Twenty years had passed since then, and though she'd left waitressing behind, she was no closer to her dream of escaping small-town life. She'd found work at the police department, replacing the previous night attendant, Cynthia Teller, who had died of a heart attack at her desk. Chief Hurley had hired Ida Lynn on the spot, captivated by her charm and quick wit—as well as other attributes. He didn't even bother interviewing another candidate.

From the beginning, Hurley had been drawn to her. There was a flirty energy between them, a casual banter that grew into something more. Hurley started with innocent touches—an arm, a shoulder—but Ida Lynn never pulled away. In fact, she welcomed the attention.

It didn't take long for things to escalate. Soon, their flirtations turned into secret rendezvous. Hurley would sneak out for long lunches, meeting Ida Lynn at her apartment, or they'd find quiet moments at the station after hours. But what Hurley didn't know was that Ida Lynn had a plan. She wasn't looking only for affection. She was looking for leverage.

Ida Lynn had arranged for a friend to hide in her apartment closet during one of Hurley's visits, snapping compromising photos of the police chief in vulnerable positions. She didn't feel proud but was done with small towns and dead-end lives. She needed an out, and Hurley was her ticket.

The photographs were damning—enough to ruin Hurley's career and his marriage. Ida Lynn planned to blackmail him for five thousand dollars. With his payment, she would have enough to get on a bus to Los Angeles, where her son had made a life. She would join him, start fresh, and leave Capetown far behind.

March 1st was the day she would show Hurley the pictures. It would be her last day on the job, her ticket to freedom. She had everything planned. Soon, Chief Hurley's world would come crashing down, and she would get what she deserved.

****

Hurley's wife entered his office, carrying a tray with his dinner. She laid it on his desk and immediately noticed his flushed face, the sheen of sweat glistening on his brow. "Danny, are you okay?" Gloria asked, her voice tinged with concern. She stepped closer and placed a cool hand on his forehead.

Hurley forced a smile, waving her off. "Yeah, yeah, I'm fine. My stomach's been acting up. Thought I might be sick, so I went to the bathroom. But I'm alright now." His tone was hurried, deflective. He was eager to change the subject. "How's little Mary feeling? Did she like the soup?"

Gloria's eyes lingered on him, not entirely convinced by his explanation, but she allowed the change of topic.

"Oh, she's fine. I think she's suffering from a little cold. Liza was worried it might be something worse, but I don't believe it is. What about you, though? Are you sure you're alright? You don't look so good." Her gaze swept the office. "And where is everyone? I only saw Ida Lynn when I came in. Usually, one of your deputies is falling all over her. You should warn those men, Danny. It wouldn't look too good if they got caught up in something with her."

Hurley chuckled, although with a little too much emphasis. "Don't worry. I've already warned them. I told each of those knuckleheads that if they cross the line, they'll be out of a job— and I won't hesitate to tell their wives either." Gloria wasn't satisfied. She tilted her head, a knowing look in her eye. "You're sure? How would you even know until it was too late?"

"Oh, I'd know," Hurley said confidently, though his words felt too rehearsed. "Those boys can't keep secrets from me. I'd sniff it out before anything got too far."

"Well, I'm glad you've spoken up. Can you imagine the chaos it would cause in Capetown? Lives would be ruined.

Think about what it would mean for you—our marriage would be over, the city council would fire you, and your dad's legacy would be destroyed. It would be devastating."

Hurley's face went pale, his eyes widening as he stammered, "Don't... don't even joke about it, Gloria. You know I'd never do something like that. I wouldn't—couldn't— hurt you or the people who depend on me."

"Good," she said, her voice firm, but her expression softened as she prepared to leave. "I wanted to make sure you understand what's at stake. Now, I'll let you eat. I hope your stomach's up for it." She reached for the door handle, paused, and added, "By the way, where did you send your men?"

Hurley breathed a small sigh of relief at the change of topic. "I sent them to Orca to handle some illegal campers. They've been gone a little longer than I expected, though. I'll check on them. Thanks for the dinner, Gloria. I'm sure it's exactly what I need."

Gloria smiled. "Don't work too late, Danny. You should be in bed if you're coming down with something." She gave him a gentle peck on the cheek and left, the sound of the door buzzer signaling her departure from the station.

As soon as she was gone, Hurley let out a heavy breath and headed toward the reception area. He tried to shake the lingering tension from his wife's words but found himself still rattled. When he approached the front desk, he gave Ida Lynn a quick smile, which she returned with a forced, almost robotic one.

Hurley frowned but let it slide. Grabbing the handheld radio, he pressed the mic button. "Buttons, where the hell are you guys? You should've been back hours ago." He waited for a response, but the radio crackled with silence. His jaw tightened as he clicked the button again. "Jenkins, Jones, Taylor—any of you with Jeremiah? Come in, dammit."

Nothing. Only static.

Hurley swore under his breath. "What the hell is wrong with those idiots? If they ever managed to do anything right, it'd be a miracle."

Ida Lynn snickered, leaning back in her chair. "I say we lynch the bunch when they finally roll in. Those four are nothing but trouble."

"Not funny," he snapped, turning to her. "Call Rob Carlton's house, see if he's there. If he is, ask him what time they got back and if he knows where the boys are. If no one answers there, try the others' homes. Let's get this sorted."

Ida Lynn sighed but reached for the phone. "I can call Rob and Paul's house, but Buttons and Taylor? They never got their new phones hooked up after the system switched over last month. Remember?" She gave him a pointed look. "Neither of them bothered to call the phone company."

Hurley's frustration deepened. "For the love of... alright, fine. Start with Rob and Paul."

She dialed Carlton's house first. After three rings, a young girl's energetic voice answered. "Carlton residence. Linda Carlton speaking."

Ida Lynn softened her voice, smiling through her words. "Well, hello there, Linda. You're so grown-up, answering the phone like you did. Good job!"

"Thank you," the girl chirped proudly.

"Is your daddy home, Linda? Chief Hurley needs to speak with him."

There was a pause before Linda's voice shrieked through the line, "MOM! IS DADDY HOME? THE BIG BOSS IS ON THE PHONE!"

Ida Lynn smirked, resisting the urge to mutter, "His big fat smelly boss, if you ask me."

After a moment, Sue Carlton's voice replaced her daughter's. "Chief, I haven't seen Rob since he left with your men hours ago. His supper's ruined, of course. This always happens when one of you needs him. Can't you find someone else to do your dirty work?" Her tone was sharp, laden with irritation.

"Mrs. Carlton, hold on for the Chief," Ida Lynn said. Before she handed the phone to Hurley, she said, "He's not there. His wife's on the phone. She says his supper is ruined because he's not back."

In a huff, Hurley took the receiver. "Hey Sue, Sorry about Rob's supper. Please have him or one of the boys call me when they return. Could you do that for me?"

"Sure, Chief, I guess so. You know, every time…"

"Thanks, Sue. I'll let you go now. Have a good night," Hurley interrupted, hanging up before she could finish.

"Oh, Brother. Okay, try Paul's phone next. If he doesn't answer, call Smitty's Saloon and the pool hall. If they're at any of those places, tell whoever answers to have them get their asses to the station. I'm going to my office to eat. Let me know what happens," Hurley said in a huff. He gave her a curt nod and started to waddle back down the hallway, his shoulders tense.

Ida Lynn watched him leave, a thin smile spreading across her lips. As his heavy footsteps faded down the hall, her thoughts turned to the photographs hidden in her closet—the ones poised to change everything. She could already picture his face when she revealed the proof of his betrayal. Hurley had no clue what was coming, and the thrill of his impending downfall sent a surge of excitement through her.

CHAPTER 28

No Escape

"That thing's following us!" Taylor yelled from the back of the truck, his voice strained and filled with dread. "And it's moving fast!" He banged on the glass window of the cab, his hand trembling. "Rob, step on it! It's right behind us!"

"Hang on, boys!" Carlton shouted. The truck came to the Centerville Road turn, and Rob took it, slowing only enough to keep the truck from tipping. The vehicle fished-tailed a couple of times before straightening out. Rudy, Taylor, and Cravenfish clung tightly, their eyes fixed on the path behind them, waiting for the creature to appear around the bend. It never did.

"Where is it?" Taylor screamed, his breath coming in quick gasps. He scanned the darkening woods to his right, expecting the monster to cut through the forest, but the thick trees and encroaching darkness made it impossible to see.

"I don't know," Wes replied. After a moment, he leaned toward the driver's side window. "Rob, don't slow down no matter what you see up ahead. Just keep going."

Carlton glanced at him, confused. "What are you talking about?"

"Tell him," Wes said, turning to Susan. "Tell him about the Indians."

Susan took a deep breath, recalling the strange encounter. "When we crashed earlier, I thought I saw three Indians standing in the road. They were dead in front of me. No way I could miss them. But when I got out of the car, they were gone—no bodies, no blood, nothing. Just... vanished. Like they weren't real. Maybe they were ghosts. I don't know. But no matter what happens or what you think you see, keep driving. Don't stop."

"That's insane," Carlton muttered, shaking his head. "There's no such thing as ghosts."

"And there's no such thing as monsters either," Susan shot back, her voice sharp. "So, what the hell killed my friends and your deputies? What is chasing us?"

Carlton didn't answer. He gripped the steering wheel tighter; jaw clenched in annoyance or maybe fear.

The sense of danger lessened as they crossed Capetown's city limits, though it didn't disappear entirely.

"Are you going to the police station?" Susan asked Carlton.

"Yeah, but I'm not staying," Carlton replied, his voice flat and distant. "I'll drop you guys and drive straight home. When I get there, I'm going to kiss my wife until she begs me to stop, hug my kids for an hour, and pray to God that thing doesn't find its way to my house. You and your boyfriend can deal with it if it does." He hesitated, then asked, "Which one is your boyfriend, by the way?"

Susan glanced at Wes awkwardly before replying, "Neither of them. Not anymore."

Carlton shrugged. "Well, if I were you, I'd pick one and find a way out of this place tonight. And never come back."

"I think that's the best advice I've heard all day," Susan said.

Carlton pulled the truck up to the police station, coming to a sharp stop. The group piled out. Without a word, Carlton sped off, disappearing down the road, eager to put as much distance between himself and whatever was chasing them.

Deputy Taylor bolted from the truck, sprinting inside. "Chief Hurley!" he yelled, his voice cracking with fear. He was pale, wide-eyed, and panting hard.

Ida Lynn, seated behind the front desk, sprang up from her chair, startled by his sudden appearance. She stumbled back, pointing toward the chief's office. "He's in there," she said, her words coming out in a rush. "What's going on? You look like you've seen a ghost."

"You won't believe it when we tell you," Wes said as he, Susan, and Rudy followed Taylor in. "But we'll wait for the chief to come out. No need to explain it twice."

Rudy, jittery and impatient, pushed past Wes. "Is there a car we can use to get out of here?" he asked Ida Lynn. His tone was sharp, on the verge of hysterical.

"Why?" Ida Lynn replied, confused. "Don't you people have one?"

"Lady, do you have a car or not?" Rudy snapped. "I'll buy it from you right now if you do. How much?"

Wes chimed in, trying to calm him down. "Rudy, you're scaring her. Let's take a minute to figure things out first."

Rudy waved him off, frantic. "You do what you want, Cravenfish. But I'm getting out of here. I mean, Susan and I are getting out of here."

Susan shot him a cold look. "Thanks for remembering me this time. But I'm afraid that train has left the station, and you're on your own now."

"What? Honey, come on," Rudy pleaded, his voice desperate. "I was scared, okay? I wouldn't have left you. You've got to believe me."

"You didn't leave her once," Wes interjected. "You left her twice. There's no coming back from that."

"Shut it, Wes, I can fight my own battles, thank you," Susan said sternly to Cravenfish. She looked at Rudy before nodding toward Wes, "What he just said."

Rudy's face flushed with embarrassment, the color rising from ashen gray to a deep red. He opened his mouth to argue, but when he saw the disgust in Susan's eyes, he snapped his jaw shut. "Whatever," he muttered. "You two stay here and play hero. I'm getting the hell out."

He turned back to Ida Lynn. "How much for the car?"

Still wide-eyed and processing the situation, Ida Lynn thought momentarily and said, "Twenty-five hundred dollars." "Is it brand new? When did you buy it?"

She scoffed. "It's a 1943 Ford, two-door. Eighty thousand miles on it. Two bald tires up front. And now the price is up to twenty-eight hundred."

"Three hundred more?" Rudy asked incredulously.

"Yep. And if you keep arguing, it'll be another three hundred."

"My God. I can't wait to get out of here. Okay, I'll write you a check," Rudy said as he reached into his back pocket."

Wes watched; eyebrows raised. "You carry your checkbook with you everywhere?"

"I do. Problem?"

Wes shook his head, a sarcastic grin tugging at the corner of his mouth. "Nope. Considering who I'm talking to, it makes sense."

"Whatever. Lady, here's twenty-eight hundred dollars. Now, hand me the keys so I can get the hell out of here."

"Is his check any good?" Ida Lynn asked Susan as she held it up to the light.

"Should be, but I'd cash it as soon as you can."

Ida Lynn opened her purse and retrieved her keys. She removed the car key and handed it to Rudy. "You're lucky. I was about to go to five thousand dollars. Figured your life was worth that much to you."

"And I'm sure he would have paid," Susan quipped.

Rudy ignored the remarks and hurried out of the station without looking back.

Just then, Hurley came out of his office, Taylor close behind. The sheriff's face was red with irritation. "What the hell is going on?" Hurley growled. "A monster? What kind of nonsense are you trying to pull?"

Susan stepped forward, her eyes blazing. "Sheriff, get your head out of your ass. Call it whatever you want: a monster, the devil, or an Indian leviathan, but something killed my people and your people. It is real, and we believe it will be here soon," Susan blazed.

"You have such a way with words," Wes said to Susan as he made his way between her and the sheriff, prompting Susan to step back. "Listen, sheriff, we don't know what it is or if it's even coming here. What we do know is that it's killed several people, and it doesn't tolerate light, especially sunlight. If we could stay here until morning, we'd appreciate it. Once the sun rises, someone can take us to retrieve our car, and we'll be out of your hair for good."

"Oh, you can stay here, alright. Taylor, lock 'em up," Hurley snarled.

"But Chief, they aren't kidding. It's exactly as I told you. There is a monster. It slaughtered Jenkins right in front of me. Bit his head clean off. And Buttons, too. We need to call the National Guard or something."

"Boy, do as I say," Hurley barked.

"Uh, Chief," Ida Lynn said as she stared out the glass door. When Hurley didn't respond, she shouted, "CHIEF!"

"What now?" Hurley snapped, already exasperated.

She pointed toward the glass door. "Look."

Everyone turned. Standing outside, an Indian in full ceremonial regalia was chanting, his lips moving rhythmically, though the words were indistinct.

Taylor rushed to the door and locked it, his heart racing.

"That won't stop it," Wes said. "The creature's always close when the Indians appear. There's some kind of connection. We need to get out of here."

Hurley scoffed. "It's some old Indian fella. What's he going to do? Now get going, all of you. I'm locking you up until I get some real answers."

Hurley started to speak, but the Indian lifted his head, his eyes glowing with a deep, malevolent red. He raised his hand, pointing at Hurley as he slowly backed away from the door.

Everyone stood frozen for a moment. Ida Lynn's voice trembled. "Did you see his eyes?"

Wes's jaw tightened. "I'm telling you. Every time that Indian appears, the creature isn't far behind. Susan, forget this idiot. Let's go."

"I'm not going anywhere, and neither are you," Hurley grumbled, though his confidence was faltering. "This is a trick. There's no such thing as monsters."

A flickering light caught Wes's attention. Outside, a small fire had appeared, casting eerie shadows against the building.

Hurley approached the door, confused. "What the hell?" He peered out. "There are three of them now—and they've got a fire going."

"The man. An Indian woman. And a little Indian girl. Right?" Wes asked.

"Yeah," Hurley said. "They can't build a fire here. Are they crazy?"

Wes shook his head. "Don't open the door."

Hurley ignored him, turning the knob and pulling the door.

Instantly, the woman and girl began to scream—an agonizing, piercing wail that rattled the nerves of everyone inside. Hurley stumbled back, startled, his eyes wide with shock. He turned to the others, his voice trembling. "What the hell is going on? Are they with you?"

When he looked back outside, his breath caught in his throat. The woman and girl's clothing were being ripped to shreds by an unseen force. Their necks sliced open, and blood was streaming from deep gashes appearing all over their bodies. A horrifying instant later, they burst into flames, consumed by fire without any visible cause.

Hurley slammed the door shut and locked it, his hands shaking uncontrollably. "I... I don't know what's going on. But something horrible just happened."

"You haven't seen anything yet. Their playmate is about fifteen feet tall with teeth like a great white shark. And if those three Indians are here, he's here too. We've got to get out of here," Cravenfish said. "Taylor, is there a way out through the back?"

"Yeah, and we've got a patrol car there. I'll grab the keys," Taylor said as he turned toward the hallway.

Ida Lynn began to tear up. "Daniel, what should we do? I'm scared."

"I'm sure there is a logical explanation for what's going on here," Hurley said. And that's when the first roar came. It shook the entire building. Ida Lynn screamed, and so did Hurley. Susan and Wes ran after Taylor, who was coming out of a room with keys in his hand. He started running, too.

"What the hell?" Hurley spouted. Ida Lynn wasn't waiting to find out. She was now scurrying toward the back door. The howl occurred again, and this time, something rammed into the side of the building. It sounded like a car or truck had crashed into the outer wall. Hurley's shoulders flew up in fright, and he began a fast-paced waddle down the hallway.

"Okay. The back door is down here," Taylor said as he made a left and then a right. When he reached the hall's end, he stopped and looked at the door.

"What the hell?" he said, reaching for the door.

"Be careful," Wes cautioned. "Open it slowly."

The door was crumpled inward, blocked by something heavy on the other side. Taylor pushed it as far as he could and peered through the small gap. "The patrol car... it's crushed. The roof's caved in, and it's been shoved against the building. We're trapped."

Wes swore under his breath. "That thing's toying with us. It wants us stuck in here."

Hurley came shuffling up, breathless and wearing a coat of sweat. It looked like he'd run a marathon instead of the fifty feet of corridor from the front to the back. "What's going on?" He gasped.

"The door is jammed by the patrol car. The monster somehow pushed it into the back of the building and up against the door. He also crushed the top of the car almost flat. No one's going to be driving that any time soon," Taylor said.

"Now what?" Susan asked.

"Like I said, time to call in the National Guard," Taylor declared as he passed everyone and ran toward the deputy's offices. The rest followed, with Hurley once again bringing up the rear.

"Now hold on," Hurley called after Taylor. "The National Guard station is in Sacramento. And even if they believed this cockamamie story, it would be hours until they could get here. It would be daylight before they arrive, and according to these brainiacs, we would be safe to go out. Right?"

"We believe so," Susan said. "But we can't say for sure."

"Well then, I say we bar the door and wait it out, whatever the hell it is," Hurley replied.

"You haven't seen it. If it wants in, it'll get in," Wes said.

"This is a police station. The walls and entry doors are reinforced, and the front door has bulletproofed glass," Hurley boasted.

"Bulletproof glass? How's that possible?" Ida Lynn said.

"Beats me, but our door has it," Hurley said. "Many stations use it now."

"I guess. But here in Capetown? Seems like a stretch," Wes said.

"Bulletproof glass has been around for a while. A colleague of mine was in Paris when some criminals damaged the Mona Lisa. The Louvre installed bulletproof glass to protect it and other priceless art pieces. But I know it's quite costly," Susan said.

"Maybe, but based on what you say is outside, you'll be glad our door is made of it," Hurley said. "I think we would be safest to stay here in the middle of the building. And if need be, the jail cells are down that hall, no more than twenty feet away. We can lock ourselves in. No way it can get through those reinforced steel bars."

"Last line of defense," Taylor mumbled.

"Not true. We also have weapons. Taylor, get the armory storage cabinet key from my desk. It's in the top left-hand drawer. If the creature somehow gets in, we'll blast it back where it came from," Hurley said and then groaned loudly like he had been punched in the gut. He bent over and began moaning.

"Are you okay?" Ida Lynn asked.

"I don't know. Maybe something I ate doesn't agree with me. Haven't felt right since we were in the…I mean, since my wife brought me my dinner."

"To be honest, you don't look so good. You're flush and sweating profusely. You should sit down for a while in your office."

There was a concussive collision, and the building shook. Seconds later, there was another thunderous thump, and several pictures crashed to the ground, sending broken glass flying in all directions. Ida Lynn let out a scream and tears burst from her eyes as if a faucet had been turned on.

The beast roared again. It was battering the outer wall in a relentless effort to get in. After the last attempt, a series of cracks raced up from above the baseboards to the ceiling left of the front door. Plaster pieces had broken free and littered the floor.

"A few more hits like that, and the wall will come down. When it does, we're finished," Taylor said.

"Is there another way out? What about the roof? Can we get up there?" Wes asked.

"Now that I think about it, there's a drop-down panel leading to the attic. We might find a way out from there," Taylor replied.

Wes nodded. "Show us."

The group rushed to the storage closet. Inside, they found a small space crammed with cleaning supplies and steel shelves. Above them, an access was set into the ceiling.

"There," Taylor said, pointing. "That should lead to the attic."

"I don't see a ladder," Wes pointed out.

"We can climb the shelving," Taylor suggested.

After the shelf closest to the panel was clear, Wes climbed up and pushed the access board aside, handing it down to Taylor. He hoisted himself into the attic, turning on a flashlight Taylor had handed him.

Wes showed it around the storage room. It was small, no more than ten feet square, and roughly six feet high. The room was empty, save for a couple of boxes in one corner. But there was a slatted ventilation opening on one wall.

"I think I've found a way out. There's a vent we can remove and climb out. I just need to see where it goes and see if there is a way we can safely go down to the street."

Wes squeezed into the space and crawled toward the vent. It was held in place by four clasping pins, which he easily released, popping the vent free. Setting it aside, he peered out and spotted a small landing platform with a ladder at the far end. He moved to the edge and looked down—the drop to the ground was about eight feet.

It would have to do. He went back inside the attic and climbed down the shelving.

"There's a vent along the outside wall leading to a ladder. Once we're out there, we're exposed. If we must leave, it'll be risky, but at least we've got an exit."

Susan, her face tense with worry, motioned for him to climb down and follow. "Good, because we're running out of time. Come take a look at this." She led Wes to the reception area, where the wall near the main door was in ruins. Deep cracks stretched from floor to ceiling, chunks of plaster scattered across the ground. The wall groaned ominously as if ready to collapse with the next heavy blow.

"A few more hits, and it will be inside," Susan said. "We need to barricade the hallway entrance, at least to slow it down while we run for it."

"I don't think anything we do will stop it once it's in here. What's working in our favor is its size. It's so massive it won't fit through the doorways. But even that might not be enough. Hey, where's Hurley?" Wes asked, glancing around.

"He's in his office. He doesn't look so good. I think he's having a medical issue of some kind," Susan said.

Wes's eyes darkened. "We better check on him. And I want to ask him some questions while we're at it."

Susan gave him a puzzled look. "Questions? Why?"

Wes hesitated, his voice dropping. "I think Hurley knows more about what's going on here than he's letting on."

They made their way toward the chief's office, but Susan stopped and grabbed Wes's arm before they entered. "Wes…"
"Yeah?"

Her speech was unsteady. "I… well, I… damn it." She took a deep breath as if preparing herself. "I promised myself I wouldn't do this again." Without warning, she rose up on her toes and kissed him—deeply, with a kind of desperate passion that caught Wes off guard.

Wes's heart pounded in his chest, and he returned the kiss with equal intensity, forgetting for a moment the danger they were in. When they pulled apart, Wes opened his mouth to apologize for his past discretions again, but Susan pressed a finger to his lips, silencing him. "Don't," she whispered, her eyes locking with his. "Not now."

Without another word, she took his hand and led him to Hurley's office.

When they entered, the sheriff was slumped forward, his face buried in his arms on the desk, his body limp. At first, Wes thought the worst.

"Uh, Chief?" Wes called out cautiously. "You, okay?"

Hurley's head jerked up, and he shot back in his chair, eyes wide with panic. "Holy Jesus! You trying to kill me with a heart attack?" He patted his chest, struggling to catch his breath. "Christ…"

"Sorry," Wes said, relieved. "But you didn't look so good there for a second. Thought you were—well, thought you were dead."

Hurley grumbled, wiping his brow. "Well, I ain't dead yet. So, did you find a way out?"

Clearing his voice, Wes said, "Yes, there is an opening in the ceiling of the janitor's closet. It leads to a vent on an outer wall, and from there, to a small landing with a ladder to the ground. We can get out of there if the creature gets inside the station. But…" Wes stopped there and stared at the sheriff.

"What's wrong?" Hurley asked, glancing down at his shirt. He tugged at the bottom, pulling it out to inspect. "Did I spill something? I'm always spilling on myself. This extra weight I'm carrying seems to be a perfect landing spot for everything."

"Well, not exactly that," Wes said, hesitating. "But your girth might be an issue if we have to use the hole in the ceiling. I'm worried you won't fit. It's a tight squeeze, even for me."

Hurley sighed, struggling to get up from his chair. "Well, guess I'll have to take a look to be sure."

When the chief stood, the phone on his desk rang, its shrill sound cutting through the tension like a blade. Hurley cursed under his breath and snatched up the receiver. "What now?" he barked into the receiver.

"Wow, twice in one night. What is going on with you?" Gloria said from the other end of the call.

"Gloria, not now. I'm in an emergency over here. I can't talk right now."

"Daniel Fitzgerald Hurley! I don't give a damn what kind of emergency you're dealing with. There's someone outside our house. I called out to them, but all I hear is this horrible moaning. I'm scared, Danny. I need you home. Now."

Hurley's face went pale. He covered the receiver with his hand and turned to Wes and Susan. "I think the thing's at my house," he whispered, panic creeping into his voice. "If it's there, maybe we can make a break for it and go out the front."

"Where do you live?" Susan asked, her tone urgent.

"Behind the station, about a hundred feet," Hurley said. "If it's in the back, we can head to the hardware store across the street or somewhere safe."

Wes thought for a moment. "Ask her if she hears anything now."

Hurley uncovered the phone and spoke in rapid fashion. "Gloria, have you heard the noise again? When was the last time?"

"What do you mean when was the last time?" Gloria's voice was frantic. "Just get home!"

248

"Gloria!" Hurley shouted louder than intended. "When did you last hear it?"

His wife pulled the receiver away from her ear and stared at it, mouth agape and wide-eyed. This outburst was uncalled for, especially with a prowler outside. She composed herself and answered his question. "The first time was about fifteen minutes ago, but I figured it was Mrs. Peterson's dog getting into the garbage again. But I remembered you stored the cans in the garage. So, I looked out the window to see if anyone was there, but no one was.

"About five minutes ago, I heard it again, but louder. And that's when I called you."

Hurley's jaw clenched. He looked at Wes. "Five minutes ago. Should we try it?"

Wes considered the risk but nodded. "It's a chance. Tell her to lock the doors and stay inside until you get there. We'll make a run for it."

"Let's go tell Ida the other two and get out of here," Hurley said.

They gathered the others in the deputy's office and explained the situation. Hurley outlined the plan: if the creature was lurking behind his house, they'd sneak out the front door and head to the hardware store across the street. Once there, they could regroup, contact people in town, and figure out how to fight back.

"You all in?" Hurley asked, his eyes scanning their faces.

Taylor nodded. "I'm in. Let's go."

Before anyone could stop him, Taylor darted toward the reception area, his adrenaline driving him forward. "Taylor, wait!" Wes called after him. "We need to make sure it's safe..."

But it was too late. Taylor had already flung open the door, stepping outside—and straight into the jaws of death.

A massive, clawed arm shot out from the shadows, grabbing Taylor by the neck. The deputy's scream echoed through the station as the monster lifted him into the air. It let out a familiar, earth-shattering roar as it clamped its teeth down on Taylor's head, biting it clean off in a single, gruesome motion.

Susan screamed, and Hurley stumbled back, his face pasty. Taylor's headless body twitched and spasmed before the creature flung it aside like a rag doll.

The thing turned its fiery eyes toward the station. "Tonight, I will fulfill my promise," it growled, its voice a deep, ancient rumble. "The last of the killers of my people will die. I will find my peace, and the Wiyots will have been avenged. You cannot escape me. Know this... come out, or I will come in."

CHAPTER 29

The Last Hurley

"GO BACK! Hurry, go back to my office!" Hurley shouted, his massive frame turning with surprising speed as he barreled down the hallway, moving like a desperate fullback trying to break through the line.

Wes, Susan, and Ida Lynn followed closely, though Ida Lynn was still gasping from the horror of seeing Taylor's head torn off.

"Oh God, what is that thing?" the receptionist wailed, her voice breaking.

Wes shot a glance at Hurley, his jaw tight. "Sheriff, what do you know about this creature that you haven't told us?" he demanded, his words cutting through the air like a knife.

Hurley spun around, incredulous. "What the hell are you talking about? How could I know anything about it? Are you crazy?"

Wes stepped closer; his eyes fierce. "Listen, your name's Hurley. Timothy Hurley was the leader of the Wiyot massacre in 1860. He and others slaughtered over two hundred men, women, and children. Every ten years since then, descendants of those who participated in the massacre have been disappearing. People from your family, Taylor's, and Jenkins's families have all gone missing. And guess what? All these disappearances have happened around the same date as the massacre."

Wes's voice dropped, brimming with intensity. "Today is February 26, 1960—one hundred years since the killings. The creature out there... it's here to finish the job. It wants to eliminate the last of the Hurleys, the final descendant of those murderers. That person is you." He jabbed a finger into Hurley's chest for emphasis. Hurley's face went pale as he stared back, visibly shaken.

"This is insane!" Hurley protested, his voice breaking. "Why should I be held responsible for something that happened a century ago? And how could this thing even know I'm related to Timothy Hurley?"

"Are you?" Susan asked, her demeanor cold and firm.

Hurley hesitated. "I was told... I was told someone in my family might have been involved in the massacre. But I never knew for sure."

Wes raised an eyebrow. "So, you had an idea but kept it quiet."

Susan stepped forward. "Did you know about strange happenings in Orca? That something was sighted there in the past—some kind of enormous beast?"

Hurley opened his mouth to respond, but Ida Lynn's voice, shaking with fear and anger, cut him off. "He knew! He knew about it!" she shouted. "He knew everything. Paul Jones told him years ago.

"Paul did a research paper on the Wiyot massacre when he was in school. He brought it up with the chief and pointed out the connection between Hurley's, Taylor's, and Jenkins's families—all of you! And you ignored it. You didn't want to hear it."

Hurley's face contorted as he wrestled with the accusation. "I didn't ignore it! I just—I didn't think it meant anything. I couldn't have imagined this."

"Too bad you didn't listen," Wes replied, his tone icy. "Maybe you could have stopped the deaths over the past few days. But now, here we are, and you're the only one left."

Hurley's lips pressed into a thin line, but he said nothing. He glanced around nervously, his eyes darting to the walls as if expecting the creature to break through any moment.

Ida Lynn's voice cut through the silence again. "It's been quiet for a while. What do you think it's doing?"

As if summoned by her words, it roared again, a deep, bone-shaking rumble, and the sound of something massive crashing into the building followed. Dust and plaster rained from the ceiling.

Wes turned to the group, his expression hard. "We need to be ready. When it breaks through, we go. We'll head for the attic, go through the crawl space, and down the ladder to the ground outside. Hurley, are you coming?"

Hurley, pale and sweating, tried to regain some composure. "Let me see this attic access you're talking about." They hurried to the janitor's closet, where Wes showed the sheriff the opening in the ceiling.

"You expect me to fit through there?" Hurley said, eyeing the hole skeptically. "I'll never make it."

"If you weren't such a fat ass, maybe you could," Ida Lynn snapped, her words dripping with contempt. "You're nothing but a useless, huge tub of lard! I'm going through it before you because if you try to go first, you'll get stuck up there like a cork in a wine bottle."

Hurley stared at her, dumbstruck, his mouth hanging open in shock. He had expected fear, panic even, but not this kind of venom from the woman he had been having an affair with for months. His voice came out weak, almost pleading. "Ida Lynn, why are you saying this?"

She glared at him, her eyes full of cold fury. "Did you really think I was sleeping with you because I wanted to? You disgust me. I only did it because I planned to blackmail you to get out of this hellhole of a town. But right now, I don't give a damn about that. I don't want to die like Taylor did, eaten by a monster while you sit here thinking you're some kind of hero!"

Tears welled in her eyes, but they weren't from sadness—just raw, seething emotion. She turned away, wiping her face as another thunderous crash rocked the building.

A heavy thump came from the reception area, followed by the unmistakable sound of concrete and timber collapsing. The beast was getting closer.

"We better go now!" Wes urged, his voice commanding. "Hurley, if you can't make it through the ceiling, your best bet is to lock yourself in one of your cells. Like you said, it's reinforced steel and should hold."

Hurley shook his head, sweat rolling down his red face. "No, I'm not hiding. I'll go with you guys. I don't want to die alone in a jail cell."

The crashing intensified. They could hear the beast tearing apart the hallway, getting closer every second.

"Let's go," Wes said, helping Susan and Ida Lynn climb through the access. Once the women were through, he turned to Hurley. "I'll go up first and try to help pull you through. Lock the door behind you—maybe it'll buy us a few seconds."

Hurley, panic rising in his chest, obeyed. He slammed the door shut and locked it. He hurried to the shelves, trying to scale up the racks. But when he put his weight on the first shelf, it creaked in resistance and then snapped. Hurley fell hard, sprawling on the floor.

"Dammit, Hurley, get up!" Wes yelled from above. He could hear the beast tearing into the office furniture, destroying everything in its path. There wasn't much time.

Hurley groaned but struggled back to his feet. He shoved the second set of shelving toward the ceiling and began to climb again. He managed to get his head and shoulders through the opening. But as he tried to go further, his massive stomach caught on the edges, wedging him in place.

"I'm stuck!" Hurley wheezed; his voice strained with panic. "For the love of God, help me through!"

Wes gripped Hurley's arms and pulled, his muscles straining. The chief's body shifted a few inches but stopped again. His face turned crimson as he gasped for breath.

"Pull harder! Please, don't leave me!" Hurley wailed, thrashing his legs in desperation.

Wes planted his feet and gritted his teeth. "On the count of three, suck in your gut and push up with your hands. Ready?"

"Yes, yes. Do it!"

"Okay. One, two…"

Before Wes could say "three," the beast roared from below. Hurley's eyes went wide, and he screamed as terror gripped his heart in a vice.

"Three!" Wes shouted, pulling with all his might. Hurley thrashed, kicking wildly, but didn't push up as instructed.

At that moment, his body shifted. For a split second, it seemed like Wes had managed to free him.

But then there was a sickening crunch.

Hurley's face contorted in pain as the beast's massive jaws clamped down on the lower half of his body. Wes's hands still held Hurley's arms as the sheriff jerked violently backward. The sound of bones snapping filled the air, followed by the nauseating squelch of flesh tearing.

Hurley's top half came free, spilling into the attic like a grotesque ragdoll—but the rest of him stayed below, ripped clean off by the creature's deadly bite.

Wes let go and staggered back, his face pale with horror.

Hurley was dead—the last of his people and the last of those who, one hundred years earlier, had destroyed the lives of hundreds of Wiyots.

CHAPTER 30

Century of Vengeance

Wes had instructed Susan and Ida Lynn to go down the ladder and, once on the ground, head to Ted Johnson's house as Hurley had suggested. He would stay and help the man through the opening, and then they would meet them. Ida Lynn said she knew the way and went out the vent and down the ladder, with Susan following behind. Neither had witnessed what had happened to the sheriff.

Wes had fallen onto his back, Hurley's severed upper half still in his grasp. The dead chief's face was twisted in terror, his lifeless eyes glaring up at Wes. Shaken, he released Hurley's arm and scurried backward. The beast roared again, but the sound was different this time—more guttural and victorious, as if satisfied with its kill.

After scrambling to his feet, Wes bolted for the vent, climbing through and down the ladder as fast as he could. His chest heaved as he reached the bottom. At least the women had made it out unharmed—he could see no sign of them. But as he jumped down the last eight feet, he heard a sickening snap. A sharp pain shot up his leg, and his ankle buckled beneath him. He had broken it.

The agony was overwhelming. Wes clenched his teeth to keep from screaming, but a low groan escaped his throat. His vision blurred as he gripped the station's wall for support, willing himself to stay upright. He tried putting weight on the injured ankle, but it was useless; the stab of pain almost dropped him to his knees.

Using the wall for balance, Wes began hopping along the side of the building, pausing at the corner to peer around. Nothing. No sign of the beast, no movement, no sound. He strained to listen—was it still inside? Why hadn't it come for him yet? Had killing Hurley been its final act of revenge? Was it over?

He waited, his breath coming in shallow gasps. The silence was eerie and unnatural. After a few nerve-wracking moments, he decided he needed to find the others.

Grimacing with every step, he hobbled across the street toward the hardware store. But before he made it halfway, a voice stopped him cold.

"Cravenfish."

Wes turned sharply, ignoring the flare of pain in his ankle. The figure of the Indian stood in the middle of the road, silhouetted by the moonlight.

"You..." Wes breathed, recognition dawning. "You were at the gas station... And again, on the road... In Orca. What the hell is going on? Are you the one killing us?"

The Indian's expression remained impassive and unreadable. "Cravenfish," he repeated, his voice low and solemn. "Thank you."

Wes blinked, stunned. "What do you mean, 'thank you'? What did I do?"

"For helping me bring the last of the murderers to justice," the Indian said, his tone as calm as if they were discussing the weather.

Wes staggered, confused. "Justice? I didn't help you do anything. I didn't know any of those people were when I got here. How could I have helped?"

The Indian's gaze never wavered. "These were the remaining descendants of those who murdered the Wiyots." His voice was emotionless, as though reciting a fact from history. "Howard. Tucker. Peterson. Taylor. Jenkins. And now, Hurley—their leader."

Wes's mind reeled, trying to make sense of it. "But they came here on their own, or they were already living here. I had nothing to do with their deaths!"

The Indian's eyes glowed in the dim light. "You are Cravenfish. Wiyot-born. Since your birth, your spirit has carried a mission."

Cravenfish froze, pain momentarily forgotten. "Wiyot born? What are you talking about? How do you know that? I don't even know my ancestry."

"You know," the Indian said. "Look inside your soul, and you will see."

Wes felt a strange chill run down his spine. Could it be true? He had never known much about his heritage, always believing he was a regular guy—just another archaeologist doing his job. But now, this revelation stirred something deep within him, something long buried.

The Indian continued. "Our work is done. We will now have peace." As he spoke, the woman and child Wes had seen earlier appeared by his side, their forms shimmering as they materialized out of thin air. The three of them bowed their heads in unison before turning and walking away, their figures fading into the night until they were gone.

****

"I don't understand," Susan said as she and Ida Lynn approached. They hadn't made it to Ted Johnson's house, having stopped behind the hardware store when the creature's rampage ended. Now, seeing Wes sitting in the middle of the road, she looked baffled. "The Indian said you're a Wiyot... and you helped him bring all of us here. Is that true?"

Wes shook his head, his brow furrowing. "Of course not... At least, not intentionally. How could I? I had no idea—none." He sat in silent thought for a moment and then added, "Did I set this in motion?"

Susan's eyes narrowed. "What do you mean? How could you have?"

Wes sighed deeply, the weight of the revelation settling over him like a shroud. "Remember when we first met? I was working for Byron Potts at the Smithsonian. After I left for Berkeley, he often called me to recommend specialists for specific projects.

"A few months ago, Byron contacted me about a dig site in Northern California—said it was connected to Native American history. There was no mention of the Wiyot or where the site was. Without thinking, I suggested you, Tank, Peggy...

and Julia. And I knew Bobby would come if Peggy were involved."

Susan's face paled as realization dawned. "Oh my God... You're saying... you recommended all of us for this? You brought us here?"

Wes stared at the ground, his stomach twisting with guilt. "I didn't know... I swear I didn't know what would happen."

There was a long silence before Susan spoke again, her voice tight with emotion. "You really didn't know?"

Wes looked up at her, his expression haunted. "I loved them. All of them. I would never have done anything to hurt them."

Ida Lynn, standing off to the side, crossed her arms. "I believe him."

Susan shot her a skeptical look. "And why's that?"

"Because he doesn't sound like he's lying. I know when someone's lying, trust me."

Susan glanced back at Wes, her eyes searching his. "Maybe... But this is still too much to take in."

Wes sighed. "I understand, but I had no idea this was what would happen. If the creature manipulated me into bringing you all here—then, yeah, that's terrifying. But it's the truth." Ida Lynn broke the heavy silence. "Do you think it's gone for good?"

Wes rubbed his injured ankle, wincing. "I think so. But who knows if it's forever?"

"At least we know what happened to the missing people," Susan said, her voice filled with sorrow. "All the people in Orca... the hunters. The relatives of the men who killed the Wiyot."

Wes nodded. "Exactly. I don't think the Orca settlers were involved in the massacre. But they were there when the creature awoke. They couldn't escape because of the gorge, and the monster slaughtered them out of sheer proximity."

Susan sighed, her eyes drifting over the quiet, abandoned streets. "It's tragic. But... at least we know."

Headlights pierced the darkness as a car pulled up to the police station. "Uh oh," Ida Lynn said, biting her lip. "That's Gloria Hurley. This is going to get ugly."

Gloria staggered out of the car, her face a mask of horror as she took in the sight of the destroyed police station. "Daniel! Daniel!" she cried, running toward the building. But then she froze, her gaze falling on Taylor's body. The raw anguish on her face twisted into something else—something darker.

"My love..." she whispered, bending down beside Taylor's lifeless form. "Daniel Hurley!" she shouted, her eyes blazing with fury as she ran into the station. "What have you DONE?!"

Ida Lynn raised an eyebrow, muttering under her breath. "Didn't see that coming. No wonder Hurley wasn't getting any at home."

Susan's face tightened. "Should we go tell her what happened?"

"Tell her what?" Ida Lynn scoffed. "How a monster ripped apart her lover and her husband? Yeah, I don't think she's going to believe that one."

Susan frowned. "Good point. But wait a minute... Hurley's son—Roger. Why didn't it kill him? He's a Hurley, too."

Wes furrowed his brow and thought for a moment. "Maybe... Roger isn't Hurley's son. Maybe he's someone else's."

A strange look crossed Ida Lynn's face as if puzzle pieces were falling into place. "Could Roger be Taylor's kid? Hurley told me he and Ed had been friends since high school. He said the three of them hung around together all the time. Could it be possible?"

"Who knows? But if Roger were Hurley's son, then I think the creature would have known and killed him too," Wes muttered. "One thing's for sure—we're never going to get the full story."

Gloria came stumbling out of the building. She staggered to her car and opened the door. Before she got in, she vomited. After wiping her mouth with the sleeve of her dress, she got in the car.

As Gloria drove away, several townspeople emerged from their homes, approaching the police station with caution. Over a dozen curious faces gathered in the street, staring in disbelief at the destruction.

"Now they show up," Ida Lynn grumbled. "I've had enough of this place. I need to get out of Capetown—now."

"I'm with you," Susan said, her voice unwavering. "Wes, how do we escape this nightmare?"

Wes glanced at Ida Lynn. "Do you still have your phone at home? Can we use it to call someone to pick us up?"

Ida Lynn nodded, a sly smile spreading across her lips. "I'll let you use it on one condition."

"What condition?" Wes asked.

"You take me with you," she replied. "I've got a check for twenty-eight hundred dollars from your jackass friend. Along with my savings, it's more than enough to start over somewhere else. Wherever you two go, I'm coming."

Wes turned to Susan, who gave a tired but affirming nod. "Sounds good to me."

"Alright then," Wes said, wincing as he stood with their help. "Let's get to Ida Lynn's house and figure out how to get out of here before anyone starts asking questions."

The three survivors, exhausted and broken, made their way down the street, leaving the horror of Capetown behind them.

CHAPTER 31

Two weeks later

Berkley, California

Wes Cravenfish's eyes fluttered open. He was in bed in his apartment in Berkley. Looking at his alarm clock, he was shocked to see it was almost 9 a.m.

"Oh shit, we're going to miss our flight. Susan, wake up," he said as he shook Susan Blake's shoulder.

"What? Why?" Susan groaned.

"Because our flights are in two hours, and we still have packing to do."

Susan bolted up. She was naked, and her breasts were exposed. Wes looked at their incredible shapes. He had to; they were beautiful. Her eyes were slits, and her hair was a tangled, crazy mess. Wes sighed, and it was a sigh of ecstasy.

He and Susan had made up, professed their love for one another, and decided to marry. That morning, they had a flight on TWA at eleven fifteen to New York City, where Susan's parents lived.

The wedding was scheduled in ten days, and there was much to do.

"Why is it so early," Susan said. "It's all your fault, you know."

"My fault?" Wes exclaimed. "Yep, if you hadn't woken me up in the middle of the night to do…well, to do *that* again, for the second time, I wouldn't have overslept."

"Well, I confess to being guilty as charged," Wes said with a chuckle. "Now get up and get going. You shower first, and I'll follow."

"You can follow me, but not until after I finish. No more of your shenanigans, Mr. Cravenfish. Oh. God," Susan moaned.

"What's wrong?" Wes asked in alarm.

"Susan Cravenfish. How am I ever going to live with that name?" Susan chuckled. She leaned over, kissed Wes on the cheek, and stood up. Wes watched her leave, once again struck by how lucky he was. Susan was stunning, with an incredible figure, but her looks weren't what made him feel so fortunate. He was in heaven because she loved him and had agreed to marry him.

The shower turned on in the bathroom, and Wes could hear Susan humming the new Elvis Presley song, *It's Now or Never*. He wondered if it was an invitation and closed his eyes, smiling. A noise jolted him out of his thoughts. His eyes flew open, and in the corner of the room stood Mad River Billy, holding a knife.

"Susan Blake," he said, "the last one."

Billy turned, raised the gleaming weapon and walked into the bathroom.

"SUSAN, LOOK OUT!" Wes yelled. "Susan, it's the killer Mad River Billy." Wes tried to get out of bed, but his ankle had a cast on it, and it was so heavy he couldn't move it. "Susan! Susan! Susan!"

"Wes, honey, wake up. You're having a bad dream again. Wake up," Susan said as she gently jostled Wes' shoulder. Cravenfish's eyes flittered open. Susan was staring down at him. "Another one of those dreams?"

"Yeah, and it was a doozy."

"Well, I hate to rush you but look at the time. We only have a few hours before we must be on in the air. My father's picking us up at the airport in New York, and we can't afford to miss this flight. No, let me rephrase that. You can't afford to miss this flight. You've used up all your allowable mistakes with my dad, so we can't screw this up."

"Oh, geez. Ok, I'm getting up," Wes said, the dream still weighing on his mind. He'd had that nightmare or others like it since they returned to Berkley. They were often debilitating and left him exhausted the next day.

Susan got up first and went into the bathroom. After a couple of minutes, Wes could hear the shower water running.

"Wes, honey," Susan called out.

"Yes, my darling."

Do you think you could come and, um, wash my back…"

Thank you for reading. Please look for other titles from the author:

The Barilla Chronicles

Severed Ties

Mission Earth

And soon,

"The Last Witness"

www.ingramcontent.com/pod-product-compliance
Lightning Source LLC
Chambersburg PA
CBHW060340310726
48976CB00003B/664